A de Luca Family Christmas Carol

Lucy Monroe

Lucy Monroe LLC

DEDICATION

For everyone who has fallen in love with the De Luca family and especially readers who like an emotional, feel good story at the holidays...mafia style. This one is for you.

ITALIAN MAFIA HIERARCHY*

G odfather of Cosa Nostra

Severu De Luca

Head Enforcer/Assassin:

Angelo Caruso

(Also known as Angel of Death)

Cosa Nostra Territories:

New York: Five Families

Bonanno (Queens), Colombo (Bronx), Gambino (Staten Island), Genovese (Manhattan), and Lucchese (Brooklyn): each founding mafia is led by a don who could be from any of the families loyal to them.

New York Genovese family

Don/Boss:

Miceli De Luca

(Also known as The Genovese and King of New York)

Underboss:

Allessio Greco

Consigliere:

Big Sal De Luca

Capos:

Domenico Bianchi

Salvatore De Luca
Tomasso Marino
Niccolo Costa
Dario Ricci
Stefano Bianchi
Las Vegas
Don/Boss:
Patrizio Mancini
Underboss:
Raffaele Mancini
Detroit
Don/Boss:
Pietro Russo
Boston
Don/Boss:
Lombard)
The Cosa Nostra is known as the Lombardi Family, despite the Americanized name for the don's family.
New England
Chicago aka The Outfit
* All names and positions are fictional or used in a fictional capacity, a product of the author's imagination, loosely based on La Cosa Nostra structure in America.

GUN CLEANING THERAPY

S AL

I slam the things I need to clean my gun on the kitchen table.
Solvent. Thwump.

Bore pole and attachments. Thwump.

Toothbrush black from use. Thwump.

None make the satisfying crack I want and I don't have the outlet of turning the air blue around me with curses. Ilaria is making the pasta for dinner.

We've always had enough money to hire staff, but she likes to cook. The first time she roped me into helping her, she ended up naked on the countertop and we both had flour in our hair and everywhere else afterwards.

The memory soothes my mood enough that each piece of my gun lands softly on the table as I disassemble my gun, movements quick and natural after three plus decades as a made man.

I've been cleaning my guns on the kitchen table while Ilaria makes pasta with her grandmother's recipe, or cannoli the way my mother did since the second year of our marriage.

Show me a man who doesn't clean his own guns and I'll show you a man ready for retirement, permanent or otherwise.

This has always been the time we took to discuss the things that matter. It's been a while since we had one of those talks.

"Is everything ok?" Ilaria lays the fresh pasta in layers of wax paper ready to boil later. "You seem a little agitated, Sal."

When did Ilaria stop calling me *caro*? Or *amato*?

I don't know, and that says more about me than it does about her.

"I'm fine," I say by rote as my mind continues to ponder the question of when my wife stopped using endearments with me.

But wrack my brain as I might, I can't remember the last time she called me *caro*, much less *amato*. Ilaria deserves better than for me not to have noticed.

My only excuse is that life has been harder since Enzo's death. After my brother died, my world shifted on its axis. Even more so than when papà and mamma passed.

Enzo was my best friend as well as my don. I miss him every day, but hell if that could come out of the mouth of the capo I was, much less the consigliere's I've become.

Besides, Enzo's son needed my support when he became the youngest don in the Five Families. Now at 36, Severu is the youngest godfather in the history of the Cosa Nostra in either Sicily or America. I'm proud of him, but I still miss the days his father was don.

Shoving my grief under a heavy workload helped to hide it from those that might see me as weak because of it, but it also cost me in my relationship with Ilaria. We aren't as close as we were seven years ago.

She nods and turns away, like she's going to leave the kitchen. There was a time she would have pushed for more, that she would have insisted I explain my bad mood.

Realizing that if I don't say something else, she's going to leave me to my gun cleaning and bad mood, I quickly say, "Everything is changing."

Including the way my wife reacts to me. What can I do to fix that?

Ilaria turns back to me, her bright blue gaze unfaded by her 53 years fixed on mine. "Life is all about change."

"My mother used to say that."

My wife's lips tilt in a small smile. "Where do you think I learned it?"

My mother adored Ilaria and Aria both, but Ilaria blossomed under my mom's approval and took her every teaching to heart.

"Some things shouldn't change," I grumble, shoving the bore cleaner into my gun's barrel harder than I need to. "Angelo is going to marry that stripper. He wants to propose at the family Christmas get together."

"He does? That's wonderful!" Ilaria's voice vibrates with delight at the prospect of our adopted nephew marrying the woman he's been obsessing over for months.

"She's a stripper, for gah..." I clear my throat. "Goodness sake."

"Have I ever told you how charming I find it that you absolutely refuse to curse in front of me?" Ilaria's smile for me is full and reaches her eyes this this time. She winks. "Except in the bedroom."

I'm not ashamed to bask in her approval. "You have, but it's been a while."

I'll never disrespect my wife in that way and it's the one area I do not allow my son or my nephews to slide either. Although, once Severu became the Don of the Genovese, I took him aside privately to remonstrate with him about cursing in front of his aunt or his mother.

I do the same for him as godfather and now that my nephew, Miceli, is my don, I extend him the same courtesy. However, I don't allow either man to slip in front of me without bringing it up later.

Their father taught them better than that.

Not that they're following Enzo's teachings in everything.

"Angelo is happy." Ilaria tsks. "You should be glad he found Candi."

"What is happy? Are we some Hallmark special? We're the mafia..." I have to bite back another set of curses. "Angelo should marry for the sake of *la famiglia*."

Ilaria's not smiling now. "Maybe that's not such an important thing anymore."

"Severu did his duty to the family, so did Miceli." Our own son, not so much.

But his marriage was ordered by his don, so there is that.

I do not begrudge Salvatore finding the love of his life, but did she have to be a former stripper too?

"Are you ever going to accept Bianca fully?" my wife asks, showing she knows what I'm thinking like she has for the past almost 35 years.

"I accept Bianca." I do.

But that my son chose to claim her when he could have married to strengthen the family is a harder pill to swallow.

"Then, if you have no trouble with our daughter-in-law's former profession, what's your problem with Candi?"

"For starters, what kind of woman calls herself a sweet? she's got a perfectly good name. Kathleen, but she insists on going by her stripper name."

"Don't let Angelo hear you calling her a stripper," Ilaria warns me seriously.

We all know how unhinged the enforcer is when it comes to his woman. The fact my wife is worried about me in the face of the younger man's wrath does not warm my heart. I can take care of myself and her, damn it.

"He prefers the term exotic dancer," she adds like that makes a difference.

"Doesn't change what she did for a living."

"No, it doesn't. Nor should it." Ilaria isn't smiling at me now. "What difference does her former job make when she's so perfect for him? Do you think a man like Angelo Caruso can find love so easily?"

"You can be happy in your marriage without being in love." That's something my father used to drill into me and Enzo.

Ilaria goes stiff. "Yes, you can. That doesn't mean I wish a loveless marriage on our son or the man as good as a nephew to us."

"Severu and Miceli love their wives," I point out.

"Yes. They got lucky."

"Like we did." I study my wife's beautiful features for a sign of what she's thinking because she sure as hell isn't saying anything.

Right now, she's more of an enigma to me than she was when we first got married. There's no soft smile like those words would have elicited before.

What the fuck is going on with my marriage?

Wiping my hands on the cloth I keep on hand for that purpose, I stand up and then stalk toward my wife. Her eyes widen and she backs up, bumping into the cabinets.

A predator's smile curves my lips.

This, at least, is as good as it ever was.

She opens her mouth to say something. In no fucking mood to hear it, I put my hands on the wall on either side of her head. Leaning down, I slam my mouth over my proper wife's parted lips.

It takes her a few seconds longer for her to melt into me than it used to but melt she does. And I shove my knee between her thighs to hold her up for my onslaught just as her knees buckle.

MARRIED...ISH

I LARIA

Sal's commanding kiss sends shards of pleasure piercing through me.

The bedroom is the only place I will tolerate being bossed around, but I more than tolerate it.

I need it.

Sal figured that out on our wedding night when his naturally domineering nature in the bedroom sent a frightened virgin skyrocketing into the stratosphere with pleasure.

34 Years Ago

My heart beating way too fast and my breath coming in short gasps, I stare at the room I've been led to.

Salvatore's bedroom in the De Luca penthouse.

Apparently, it's De Luca family tradition that the men spend their wedding night in the family home, a penthouse that takes up two floors at the top of a an art deco building they've owned since it was built in the 1920s.

However, we won't be living here, like Enzo and Aria, my new husband's brother and sister-in-law.

My father has gifted us a building too. And the penthouse suite has been designed for us to live in. We'll eventually inherit the house on Long Island I grew up in along with all my father's other assets. And I do mean *we*. Sal will inherit right along with me, just as he will inherit my father's position of capo.

Unlike so many other things in my life, including the man I would marry, I was consulted on the colors and the furniture for my new home.

Tomorrow, we leave for our honeymoon in Sicily. Where my husband will be meeting with leaders in the Italian Cosa Nostra on behalf of his father, Don Matteo.

Some honeymoon, right?

"You look beautiful." Sal's deep voice washes over me, sending sparks of sensation along my nerve endings.

Or maybe that's just terror.

"Even Quasimodo would look good in this dress." I turn to face Sal with a swish of silk.

Made in Milan, like all the best wedding dresses, according to mamma, the yards and yards of white silk and lace encasing my body is the height of 80s couture.

Poofy sleeves of hand tatted Sicilian lace narrow to fit tightly around my forearms and brush the top of my hands. The crinoline underneath the skirt has so many layers, there are two feet between the tips of my toes and the hem of the overskirt.

The train is not quite as long as Princess Di's when she got married, much to my mom's chagrin. But I seriously don't know if the bustle created by the ruched up train, cleverly attached to the back of my dress would work if there was an inch more silk to contend with.

"I'm glad you didn't change out of the wedding dress for the reception." Sal's hot gaze sends those butterflies pinwheeling again.

"You can thank my mother for that." She could hardly brag about the handmade ten-thousand-dollar wedding gown to all the other capo's wives if I wasn't wearing it.

"I'd rather show my appreciation to you."

Did he really just say that?

My new husband.

How many times have we spoken? Ten, maybe fifteen, in all the years we have both been part of the Genovese Family.

Now, he's making sexual innuendos and looking at me like I'm a plate of spaghetti and he's a starving man.

Because I'm his wife and our lives are joined forever. It might be the 1980s in the rest of the world, but it's still the 16th Century in the mafia when it comes to divorce.

It's not an option.

Just like *la famiglia* itself, the only way out of a mafia marriage is death.

King Henry VIII style.

An image of my own lifeless body, head severed and resting in a gory pool of blood, flashes into my brain.

I can't breathe and try to suck in air, only my corset's too tight. It was fine ten minutes ago, but now it squeezes my ribcage like a hungry boa constrictor.

"You sound like you're about to hyperventilate." Sal's gray gaze glints with humor.

I'm glad one of us finds this situation amusing.

"It's the corset." It's so not the corset.

I'm about to have sex for the first time. Not with the man I love. I'm not in love with anyone, least of all the stranger I just married for the sake of mafia business.

Said mafia being stuck in the 16th Century in more ways than one, as a woman, I cannot inherit the capoship from my father. That means marrying someone who can.

That man is Salvatore Tomaso De Luca, second son of the don and fully made man.

He's got Al Pacino's dreamy looks with Arnold Schwarzenegger's muscles and six-foot-two-inch height. A total dreamboat, but still a stranger.

Only three years older than me, he exudes a worldly cynicism my nineteen-year-old self only aspires to.

He smirks. "The corset. Sure. We'll go with that."

We'll see if he's still laughing when I throw up from nerves.

"It's different for you," I accuse.

Of course, he's taking what's about to happen in stride. He was raised to be a mafia soldier. I was raised to be a mafia princess.

He's experienced. I've never been kissed.

If the rumors are true, he got made when he was sixteen, killing someone for the mafia and taking his vow to the Cosa Nostra.

I've never raised my hand to another person.

He just graduated college with a degree in business. It's the new mafia where the made men who want to be somebody get an education.

I wanted to go to college. I knew my parents expected me to marry someone to become my father's heir but that didn't mean my whole life had to be about that.

Only to them, it did.

Papa's not proud of my intelligence. Mamma is unimpressed by my ability to analyze and use critical thinking skills. But both are really happy my uterus is in working order.

Yes, they had it checked. For real.

But when it came time for mamma to give me a talk about the birds and the bees, suddenly she's too circumspect to talk details. She literally said Sal would know what to do and to go along with it.

Whatever *it* was.

Looking at him right now, I believe he knows his way around the bedroom. Doesn't make me any less nervous.

He shrugs. "Sure."

"You're as inspiring as mamma," I complain. "She told me not to worry. It's not that terrible."

Sal barks out a laugh. "That's not much of a recommendation for sex."

"That's what I thought." I didn't say that to mamma though.

Doing so would have gotten me a smack to the back of my head. Mamma is ladylike in public but behind closed doors, she rules with an iron fist, and I am the one she's been ruling for the past 19 years.

"I'm not your dad."

"That's a good thing because eww."

He smiles. "You're funnier than I expected."

"You mean I have a brain?" Anger at the pigeonhole my life has been forced into settles some of the butterflies dive bombing in my tummy. "I'm not just an arm accessory with a uterus."

"No, you are not." There's not a speck of humor in his tone or expression now.

I'm not feeling all that amused myself. "I could do with another glass of champagne."

Technically, I'm not supposed to be drinking at all. I'm not of age.

But this is the mafia.

I can drink champagne, but heaven forbid I kiss a boy before marriage. Bitter laughter chokes in my throat and I have to bite it back.

"What's funny?" Sal asks.

"Nothing," I say with all honesty.

Nothing about this is funny. Terrifying? Check. Embarrassing? Check. Funny? Not so much.

"Do you need help getting out of your dress?" It's a question, but from the look on his face, there's only one right answer.

"Yes. I'm trussed up like a Thanksgiving turkey in this thing." And like that sacrificial bird, I've got no hope of getting out of it.

"I'm surprised your mother didn't want to help you with this."

"Your family has its traditions," I say referring to us having our wedding night in his family home. "Mine has ours."

"Me helping you out of the dress is one of them?"

I nod.

Possessiveness and sexual desire gleam in his eyes just like they have ever since our engagement was announced. "I like this tradition."

"I'm glad somebody does," I mutter.

Even if I'd wanted to change into a nightgown, mamma made sure the design of my dress makes it impossible for me to remove myself.

There are thirty-two tiny silk covered buttons going from the top of my neckline all the way to my butt. They're hard enough to undo when you can see them, but I'd have to be a contortionist to get them undone on my own.

If the buttons aren't deterrent enough, my tightly laced corset is secured with a double knot. That's to encourage Salvatore to use his knife to cut the laces.

It's supposed to symbolize something, but I don't know what. I tuned my mom out right after she told me I wouldn't be able to undress myself on my wedding night.

Sal steps forward. "Turn around."

I don't move.

"I am not going to hurt you, *cara*."

"If you do, I'll shoot you in your sleep. Just so you know." I am not one of those mafia women who will tolerate being beaten on by the man she's married to.

Instead of anger flashing in his gorgeous gray gaze, respect flashes in Sal's eyes. "The De Luca men do not hurt those they are meant to protect."

"Are you saying you won't beat stoicism into our son?" An ember of hope for a different life than the ones my parents planned for me kindles in my heart.

"You do not teach strength by behaving with weakness."

It's not the answer I expect, but it's everything I want to hear.

"Promise me, Sal," I fervently demand.

"I give you my vow as a made man. I will never beat our children."

Something loosens inside of me and that ember flickers into a flame. "Thank you."

"Now, turn around." There's no give in his tone.

That's a clear demand and his expression says he expects me to obey.

"What if I don't want to?" I have to ask.

It's all well and good to make a promise. Every made man in *la famiglia* vows fidelity on his wedding day, but more have broken that promise than kept it.

My father included.

"Are you going to deny me on our wedding night?" he tosses back at me.

"I want to know if you'd let me."

"Yes." He doesn't hesitate to answer.

But the front of his slacks is tented, making it impossible to miss how aroused he is. That bulge fascinates me but I drag my eyes up to his, looking for the truth. He's as enigmatic as any made man. Can I trust him?

I wonder how many mafia princesses wonder the same thing on their wedding nights.

Taking a leap, I believe. "Thank you. And the answer to *your* question is *no*. I'm not going to deny you."

No matter what either of us wants, this is going to happen tonight because we have to present the bloody sheets to the families tomorrow. I'm lucky that I at least feel desire for my new husband. I've heard the whispers from the women who don't.

"I'm glad." His sexy smile sends tingles through my nether regions.

And I'm glad Sal so obviously wants me.

"I don't want our children to have to present the sheets in the morning." I hate that barbaric practice, but I still don't expect the words to come popping out of my mouth.

On my wedding night no less.

Why tell him that? Sal's old-school and it's only going to cause division between us. And our children aren't even born yet.

"You want to make changes in *la famiglia*?"

In for a penny, in for a pound. Right? "When it comes to personal dignity, to women being valued for more than the tightness of their hoo-hah on their wedding night? Yes."

"Hoo-hah?" He rolls his eyes. "Your *pussy* will be tight every time we make love because I'll make it so swollen with pleasure only your slick juices will make it possible to get my dick inside you."

"Sal!" Heat rushes through me at his dirty words.

"In our bedroom, we don't play roles. You aren't the perfect mafia princess. I'm not your dad's underboss. Sex is earthy and we're not starting our marriage with hangups about it."

"Glad you said that. Your words just made my nerves disappear like *poof*." Snapping my fingers, I roll my eyes.

"I will not ask for the presentation of the sheets,' he says, ignoring my sarcasm. "Not for our daughters and not for the women who marry our sons. I cannot control the actions of others, however."

"You're a De Luca. You can be very persuasive." And I don't mean charming, though he is that too.

De Luca men are the scariest charmers in New York. Probably the entire country.

"Yes, I can." Sal's voice is laced with sensual threat as he walks with panther like grace around me. Stopping inches from my back, he lays his hands on my shoulders. "Whatever our children's future, *we* have to present the sheets tomorrow."

"I know." There's no keeping how much I hate that knowledge out of my voice.

Making love for the first time should be private. Personal.

But the evidence of our joining is going to be displayed for all the guests at the wedding breakfast to examine and give witness to the consummation of our marriage.

It's like we're really royalty...from another century.

"I can fake the blood if you would rather wait."

Butterflies swoop and dive inside my tummy. Is he for real?

My estimation of Salvatore De Luca, new underboss to my father but apparently my husband first in this moment, goes up a thousandfold.

"I would rather just get it over with."

Sell chuckles ruefully. "That's a ringing endorsement of desire right there."

I try to turn, but his hands hold me in place.

So, I have to speak toward the bed and not the man behind me. Maybe that's easier for this burst of honesty.

"It's not that I don't want you. I think you know I do, but I'm afraid and I'd rather not give that fear time to grow." I'm hoping tonight will be good enough to alleviate it all together.

"Whether we do this tonight, or on our honeymoon, I promise I will do my best not to hurt you."

"What about the tradition of spending your wedding night in the family home?" I ask.

"We'll spend the night here. No one can force us to have sex if we don't want to." He's pressed up against my back and the hard ridge pushing into my spine is evidence that he wants sex with me.

It's my desire he's showing so much consideration for.

Sal is giving me a choice.

And I choose to put my body in his hands.

Before I can tell him that, he leans down and speaks softly directly into my ear. "I've never been to bed with a virgin before, but I asked around and I know I can make it good for you."

"You asked around?" That's kind of amazing. A made man asking for direction in the bedroom. "I thought you were more old school than that."

"Traditions are important to me, but so is my wife."

Emotion shudders through me at his words. *I matter to him*. Me.

Not because he can use me to further his own ends, but because he takes being married as seriously as I do.

I cross myself.

"What was that for?"

"It's a miracle. You're a miracle." Because of Sal, Ilaria De Luca has value where Ilaria Benetti was nothing more than a pawn my father was happy to dispose of.

"I've been called the devil, but never a miracle before." His tone is amused.

But I don't care. I know what I feel, and right now it's a lot more emotion than I expected to for the stranger I married.

"Then make it good for me."

OOPS, THAT WAS HOT.

S AL

Make it good for me.

There's a hidden sensuality in Ilaria that calls to the primitive man inside me. The one who needs to conquer and claim.

Not an enlightened 80s man, but what made man is?

Her dress brushes against my fingertips as I slide my hands to the row of tiny buttons holding the bodice in place. No chance anyone believed my bride could get herself out of this dress.

Ilaria is wrapped up like a present that only I can open. My already hard cock pulses with the need to be buried in her tight pussy.

Undoing the top few buttons, I say, "I'm going to make it so good, you're going to need a cushion to sit on tomorrow."

Goosebumps erupt on her exposed skin and I smile. My new wife likes my dirty talk.

Leaning down, I inhale her scent. Soft floral mixes with sandalwood and musk. "Fuck, you smell good."

"It's Red Door. Mamma gah..." Ilaria's voice hiccups as I press my lips against her nape.

"She got a bottle for me before the launch."

Nuzzling the skin under her ear, I inhale more of her tempting scent. "Whatever it is, it's perfect on you."

My mom only wears Chanel No. 5, but she's from that generation. She refuses to try anything new because she insists that once a woman finds a fragrance that mixes right with her own body chemistry, she should stick with it.

I'll keep Ilaria supplied with Red Door from now on.

As I undo more buttons, I get a peek at what she's wearing under the wedding gown fit for the mafia princess she is. I don't expect the white satin corset edged in lace to be tied in a fucking knot at the top.

Fuck me. "The only way I'm getting you out of this corset is to cut the ribbons."

"That's what you're supposed to do," Ilaria says breathlessly.

I approve. "These Benetti traditions are sexy as hell."

"I'm glad you think so."

"You don't?"

"I didn't this morning when mamma and the designer trussed me up like this."

"And now?" I breathe against her ear.

She shivers like I expect her to.

"I'm pretty sure anything with you would be sexy," she says like the idea surprises her.

"Good." Because I have plans.

Not typical plans for a wedding night with a virgin, but Ilaria isn't just an innocent bride. She's *my* bride and that streak of sensuality running under the surface is going to make her my perfect lover, just like I will be hers.

"Thank you." Her soft voice rings with unexpected emotion.

I'm not sure what she's thanking me for though. "For what?"

"For giving me a reason to be grateful for my wedding night."

"How?" I haven't done anything yet except undo a few buttons on her dress and promise to destroy the ribbons on her corset with my knife.

"By showing affection and not just sexual need."

Is that what this is? Affection? When Capo Benetti approached my father about the marriage deal, I didn't think of Ilaria as a person, but the means to an end. That changed quickly on the night we announced our engagement. Another man flirted with my fiancée and I quietly took him aside.

He went home with a busted jaw and the promise of death if he got too familiar with Ilaria again. Within twenty-four hours every soldier in the Genovese Family knew to keep their distance from my future wife.

However, they weren't the only ones who had to keep their distance. Ilaria and I barely saw each other during the months before our wedding. I spent a lot of that time in Italy on mafia business for my dad. And hers.

When I *was* in New York, no private dates were allowed.

Her father saw the way I looked at his daughter and assumed there would be no blood on the sheets if we had time alone together. I can't be sure he was wrong.

My dick has gotten hard for one woman in the last year and it's the one who just told me to make it good for her.

"You didn't dismiss my fear either," she adds before I figure out what I want to say about the affection thing. "And you made promises about our future that, if you keep, makes it shine a lot brighter than it was for me this morning before we spoke our vows."

"I'm a De Luca. I always keep my promises." Knowing she wasn't looking forward to our future together as much as I was makes me determined to prove to her how good we can be together.

"Thank you," she says again.

Shaking my head where she cannot see, I undo a few more buttons. It feels like there's a hundred of them. "Don't thank me for being decent to you and having honor."

I like that she thinks I'm something special. A man wants to be larger than life in his wife's eyes. But I don't like that she thinks she has to show gratitude for what should be a given.

My father raised Enzo and I with a harsh hand, like all made men with their sons, but he showed by example how to revere the women in our family.

"Papà would skin me alive if I did not treat my wife with the respect and consideration you are due," I tell Ilaria truthfully.

I don't know if my father loves my mother, but he's always treated her with respect and care. The mafia might come first, but that doesn't mean she comes last.

"Your parents are the couple my mom threw in my face as proof of how well an arranged marriage could work."

Interesting that the Benetti's own marriage wasn't enough to convince her. "Did they have to convince you of the arrangement?"

My cock is hard enough to pound nails through concrete and my bride is telling me she had to be convinced to marry me.

Unwilling to examine why the idea she's not entirely happy with this marriage creates a lead ball in my gut, I undo two more buttons.

This is the mafia. We all do our duty.

"If by convince you mean my father reminding me that I am no more immune than any other member of the mafia when it comes to loyalty, then yes."

Dannazione. God-fucking-damn-it.

My hands stop on the last button. "You didn't want to marry me? They forced you?"

I refuse to consider what form that punishment would have taken right now. I don't want to have to kill my father-in-law on my wedding night, but we will have words about threatening Ilaria.

He will never do it again.

She is mine to protect now.

"It's not you I objected to, Sal. That has to be obvious. I knew I wasn't going to fall in love with Prince Charming and get married on a puffy pink cloud of dreams." She sighs. "But I wanted to go to college."

Relief out of proportion to her words sends more blood surging to my dick. "You still could."

"You don't mean that."

Leaning down, I kiss the join of her neck and her shiver pleases me. "You will learn, *cara*, that I never say anything I don't mean."

"Oh." She turns fast, her voluminous skirts wrapping around her legs, and looks up at me, beautiful blue eyes luminous. "You'd really support me going to college?"

"Yes."

"But what if I get pregnant right away?"

I don't bother saying we can use birth control. We can't. This is the mafia. Children are expected.

"Then you take time off and go back after the baby's born. Two of the seven women in my MBA program were nontraditional students in their thirties."

Her mouth slackens in shock. "There were seven women in your program?"

It might be the 80s, but women in master's program focused on business are almost as uncommon as female students in the engineering, or science departments.

"Yes."

"Then—"

Done with talking about how much she didn't want to marry me, I kiss my beautiful bride and cut off the gratitude I don't want to hear either.

Ilaria doesn't melt. She goes nuclear, her lips eating at mine as hungrily as I devour hers. I shove the dress down her body, the last button ripping away under my impatient fingers.

She grabs two fistfuls of my shirt and holds on like that's all that's keeping her up.

My hands are everywhere, caressing Ilaria's incredible body through the satin corset. But there are layers and layers of silk still covering her from the waist down. Ripping at the binding in the back, satisfaction fills me at the sound of the zipper giving way so I can shove the poofy slip the rest of the way off.

The layers of white land in a heap around her feet and ankles with a soft rustle. My roaming hands find her hips and deepening the kiss, I lift her up against me.

With a sexy little mewl, she wraps her legs around my body, pressing her pussy against my torso and giving me access to her luscious ass.

I take a handful and squeeze. She moans rubbing her sex against me.

Fuck. She's so sexy.

Sliding my hand over her ass and between her thighs, I press my middle finger against her sweet spot, giving her something to rub against.

She cries out against my mouth and moves her hips frantically until her body goes rigid and my innocent wife gives herself an orgasm rubbing off on me.

Stepping over the pile of silk, I carry her to the bed. I lean down and rip the bedding away and lay her down on the mattress.

Looking luminescent against the black satin sheets, in her white corset, garter and stockings, Ilaria looks up at me, her gaze hazy with passion. "You're still dressed."

"We'll get to that."

ILARIA

I don't ask what comes first. Because it's obvious.

Me.

Sal rubs his middle finger under his nose, inhaling. "Your arousal smells so good. I can't wait to taste it."

Heat climbs my neck and into my cheeks. That's the finger I rubbed so hard against. But he can't mean what it sounds like.

I've heard the gossip in the girls locker room at school. I know that some boys put their mouth *there*. Not mafia men though. Not a made man. He would never do that.

My body doesn't get the message my brain is sending because I feel a gush of moisture between my legs at the thought of Sal's mouth between my legs.

"Get up on your knees and turn away from me," he orders in a guttural voice.

Despite having just had the best orgasm of my life, my core throbs with renewed desire at my new husband's commanding tone and the hungry look in his eyes.

Yes, I've touched myself. This is the 1980s, not the 1880s. But no climax I've ever given myself felt like *that*.

Wishing I knew how to make this look sexy, I awkwardly maneuver myself to my knees. My back to Sal, I kneel at the edge of the big bed.

He's going to cut off my corset. Shivers cascade down my spine in anticipation.

I'll be left in nothing but my lace panties, a garter belt and silk stockings. They're the exact color of my skin and so sheer, they're all but transparent. Don't ask me how mama found them.

But if you don't see the band at the top of each stocking, it looks like my legs are bare.

My shoes are on the floor somewhere with my dress. They fell off when I was rubbing against Sal like a horny cat. That should embarrass me, but all I want to do is purr and do some more rubbing.

Sal groans. "You have a beautiful ass, *cara*."

"That's the way you speak respectfully to your wife?" I flirt.

Reaching down, he cups both my butt cheeks and squeezes. "Nothing I say in the bedroom will ever be intended as disrespect, but it is the one place I will use that kind of language around you. This is not a place for polite masks."

I realize I don't want any masks between us at all.

Is that even possible in a mafia marriage?

"No masks in the bedroom," I agree.

He kneads my bottom sending frissons of pleasure down my thighs. "Ready?"

"For what?" Are we having sex like this for the first time?

His big hands drop away from my backside and then a snick sounds on my left. I turn my head and see a switchblade gleaming sharply in Sal's hand.

"Don't move," he orders. "I don't want to cut you."

The flat of the blade slides over my shoulder and down my spine. I know how sharp men in our world keep their knives. If he slips, even a little, Sal will cut me.

But there is no fear inside me. Only excitement.

The knife lifts from my skin and there's movement at the bottom of my corset. His knife is so sharp, I don't hear the silk ribbons being cut, but my corset falls away from my body.

Exposed to the air, my nipples tingle and pucker more tightly.

I'm not big on top like some of my girlfriends. The corset was designed to push my B cup boobs into prominence and give me cleavage I wouldn't normally have.

Will Sal be disappointed with the real thing?

The knife drops onto the bed and his hands come around to cup my modest curves. "Mine," he growls.

"I belong to myself." The words are right.

I know they are, but something about them feels wrong.

"You belong to me and I belong to you, Ilaria. No other man will ever touch you like this." He kneads my breasts like he's not disappointed by their size at all.

"And no other women for you."

"The De Luca men are faithful in marriage," he reminds me, pinching my nipples.

Gasping, I sway forward, only his hold on my chest keeping me in place.

He flips me around and onto my back, his hungry gaze devouring me as he arranges me just so on the slippery satin bottom sheet. It slides sensually against my skin and the urge to purr and rub grows.

Picking up his knife again, his molten gaze zeroes in on the apex of my thighs. "You're so wet, your panties are soaked through."

Should I be embarrassed? I'm not. "It's your fault."

His grin is all satisfied male. "Yes, it is."

He picks up his knife and reaches toward me. There's no urge to move away from the sharp blade. He won't hurt me.

"Don't move," he warns me a second time before sliding the knife blade between my skin and the silk of my underwear.

A second later, he's cut the other side as well and he pulls my panties away from my body, leaving every intimate part of my body exposed to him.

"So beautiful," he breathes almost reverently and then he pushes my thighs wide. "Such a pretty pussy."

I choke on a laugh. "I don't think there's such a thing."

"Trust me, *cara*, there is and yours is the prettiest."

Why does hearing that turn me on so much?

There's no time to ponder the question before he lowers his head and puts his mouth right *there*.

"Sal!" What is he doing?

He ignores me and licks me, the tip of his tongue swirling around my pleasure spot.

"Oh, gah..." My voice chokes off as something hard presses against my entrance.

His finger. It has to be. But when he pushes inside my slick channel, it feels too big to be a finger. I never noticed he had giant hands before, but...

My thoughts splinter as he presses that thick finger upward and touches something with a direct current to every other nerve ending in my body.

Ecstasy builds so fast, my climax hits before I even know it's on the horizon. My scream shatters the air around us. He keeps doing what he's doing until tears of pleasure wash down my temples and my body goes limp.

Sal surges up and tears out of his clothes, removing his tuxedo shirt, jacket, cummerbund, and bowtie. As each item of clothing is removed, my breathing grows faster until I'm practically panting.

Sal De Luca has an amazing body.

My mouth goes dry at the site of my husband's naked torso. Dark curly hair covers his chest trailing down the center of his sculpted abs.

When his hands go to the waistband of his slacks, I hold my breath.

I have only ever seen a naked man, in a playground magazine, one of the girls brought to school with her. It got confiscated and she spent a week in detention, but the rest of us were more than a little grateful for the opportunity to see something we were probably never going to see until our wedding night.

Sure, some of the girls at the school were sexually active. But us mafia princesses? We knew that having sex before marriage could be risking more than our reputations.

It would have been seen as dishonoring both our parents and our capos and dons. That kind of dishonor could end in death. Or being married off to some geriatric mafioso over in Italy.

I was never going to risk that happening.

Sal pulls his boxers away from his body and over his engorged erection. It's so much bigger than the ones I saw in the magazine, my air rushes out of me in a shocked gasp.

"There's no way that's going to fit inside me." Has he seen my vagina?

"I'll fit." His face is near demonic with lust, his naked body lands on top of mine a second later. Then it's not his finger pushing against my virgin opening. "I'm going to make you mine now."

All I can do is nod.

I want this. No way can I orgasm again, but my body craves his closeness more than it does chocolate that time of month. Way more.

He presses inside, the rigid set to his jaw proof of how tightly he's holding onto his desires. Something deep inside me melts.

Using short thrusts, his body invades mine inch by slow inch. He's breathing like he just finished the Boston Marathon by the time his pelvis presses against my own.

But there is no tearing pain. I'm stretched more than I knew my body could stretch down there. I'm so full, I swear he's occupying space I know is anatomically impossible.

He starts to move, thrusting in and out of me at an excruciatingly slow pace and my passion begins to rise again.

I squirm my lower body, seeking more and Sal grips my hips, taking control of my movements. He guides me at the pace he wants, keeping me at the angle he wants and I let him.

More than let him, I revel in the freedom of not having control.

"You're going to come on my cock," he grits out, his desire burning down at me from his eyes.

"I can't come again." From what I heard from other girls at school, I'm lucky I came at all, much less twice.

"You can and you will." His guttural tone promises he won't accept any other outcome.

Then there's no more talking. Sal plunges in and out of me like a jack-hammer, forcing pleasure into my exhausted body until I'm riding toward another impossible climax.

When I come this time, I scream so loud it hurts my throat. Sal ruts a few more times and then goes rigid above me, filling me with his essence as he shouts my name and inscribes his indelibly on my heart.

AFTERGLOW & SASS

What feels like hours later, I become aware of how the pins from my updo are digging into my head, but I don't want to move.

This closeness with Sal is unlike anything I've ever felt before. Like I truly belong for the first time in my life.

Inevitably, Sal withdraws from my body and I have to stop myself grabbing for him to keep him close.

Wetness gushes from me and I wince.

"What's wrong?" he asks. "Do you hurt? I took you pretty hard at the end."

He really, really did. But I'm not complaining. "It's messy and there's going to be a wet spot."

"I'll have the sheets changed while we're bathing."

"What? No. You can't."

But I learn that Sal isn't affected by embarrassment like normal people. He can and does call for a maid to come in and change the sheets before carrying me into the bathroom.

Sitting me on the toilet, he orders me to pee.

"Excuse me?" I could not have heard him correctly. "Did you just tell me to go pee?"

"Yes."

"I'm not a child, Sal."

"No, you are my wife and it is my job to take care of you. Peeing after we fuck will decrease your chances of getting a bladder infection, but I want you to drink cranberry juice for breakfast every morning too."

"What the heck? Do you think you're my doctor?"

"I know I'm your husband."

"That doesn't make you the boss of me." In the mafia, it kind of does but I don't want that kind of marriage.

"You like me telling you what to do when we fuck."

"And I like you using that word with me in private, but if you do it in front of other people, I'll put soap in your spaghetti."

He grins. "Noted. I won't boss you around in public unless it has to do with your safety."

That's such a huge concession, it leaves me breathless. "If you mean that, I'll do my best never to argue with you in public either."

As a well trained mafia wife, that should be a given, but I don't care.

He nods, like it's a done deal and the melting place in my heart is the size of a lake right now.

"Now, pee," he orders again.

"Do married people really do that? Pee in front of each other?" I ask, unable to imagine my mother allowing my father into the bathroom with her while she puts her makeup on, much less empties her bladder.

And that thought right there is what makes me release my bladder. I don't want a marriage anything like my parents.

After I pee and use the bidet, I stand in front of the mirror, feigning a nonchalance I do not feel, and start pulling the bobby pins from my hair.

"Stop," Sal demands. "I'll do it."

"You'll do it?" He wants to take out my hairpins?

Sal nods and reaches for my head, his fingers gentle as he removes each pin. Long tresses, sweaty from our lovemaking fall around my face in messy waves.

I grimace.

"Did I hurt you?" he asks.

"I'm a mess." Nothing like the put together woman I was raised to project.

Sal runs his fingers through my hair making sure there are no snarls. I have to blink away tears at the tender care he takes with me. No one has been this gentle with me since I was a little girl.

Mamma has always been from the old school of mafia women who don't show emotion and expect their daughters to do the same. But until her father and brother were brought up on RICO charges, she loved me. She says women have to learn to live with the hard knocks in life gracefully.

What she really means is stoically.

I was born the year the RICO Act passed and a child when so many of our men went to prison. Everything was chaos. We were all scared, but Mamma and the other women in *la famiglia* reacted with courage and stoicism, bringing calm to the chaos.

Only, for her and a lot of her peers, that stoicism leaked over into their family lives. Some of us were born to loving mammas that turned into the keepers of tradition and mafia life as one man after another went to prison. She withheld warmth and softness in the name of teaching strength.

I may have lost mamma's love as a little girl, but I don't want to live my adult life without tenderness. And the way Sal is treating me says I don't have to.

He may not love me, but he's not afraid of showing me the affection my thirsty heart is aching for. At least behind the closed door of our bedroom.

"You're beautiful." After Sal's finished detangling my hair, he massages my scalp.

I would argue with him about being beautiful when I look like such a mess, but I'm too busy moaning with pleasure. His strong fingers rub away the tension from my wedding day and the weeks leading up to it.

"You like that?" he asks in a tone that says he already knows the answer.

I'm not about to give him everything on a platter. "I don't hate it."

Sal DeLuca may be a god in the bedroom, but he is going to have to work for it with me. Because I want a marriage, where he makes an effort, not just me.

"Faint praise from a woman practically in a puddle from how much she likes what I'm doing," the mafioso teases me.

I wink at him in the mirror. Me. *I* wink. Like flirting isn't something I've tried for the first time on my wedding night. "Got to keep you on your toes, Mr. De Luca."

"Call me husband."

"You're pretty possessive for a guy who didn't even court me, *marito*."

His eyes flare with approval when I call him husband like he wants. "I'll court you now that we're married. Your father and mother gave me no access to you in the last year."

"I didn't know that." They kept us apart? "Why would they do that?"

"Probably because your father saw the way I looked at you and knew there would be no bloody sheets the morning after our wedding if we had time alone."

"That's pretty presumptuous of you." But a thrill of desire zaps me.

He wanted me. Not just for the contract so he could become capo one day, but me. Ilaria, the woman.

"After what just happened, are you denying it?"

I shrug. "This is our wedding night."

"It is." Sal turns me so I'm looking into his handsome face directly. "Our marriage may be the result of a mafia merger, but that does not mean we weren't created for each other. You were destined to be mine."

"Are you religious?" I am a good Catholic girl.

I took my catechism classes. I memorized all the things I'm supposed to. But do I believe all of the church's teachings?

No.

There are too many things that do not make sense to me. Like women having to submit to men, even when they're being physically abused. That feels like something men made up and put into the Bible if you ask me.

Mamma would have a heart attack if I said something out loud like that, but I have a feeling Sal might even agree with me.

INSERT EMOTIONAL DAMAGE

S AL

The Present

Our lovemaking is incendiary. After sitting my wife on the edge of the counter, I eat her sweet pussy until the dulcet cries of her release ring in my ears.

Then I shove her thighs wide and plunge inside, reveling in her tight, slick heat, like I have every single time we've made love for the last three and a half decades.

We're dressing again after our second shower of the day and I'm feeling more content than I have in a long time.

Ilaria finishes doing her hair, the final erasure of the evidence of what we did in the kitchen.

"Sometimes, I wish you'd just leave it down." The only place she allows herself to get messy as she calls it is in the bedroom and her ceramics studio.

Ilaria went to college like she wanted once Salvatore started school, but studied for a fine arts degree and made ceramics her art form of choice.

My wife faces me with the look she gets when she's about to ask or say something I'm not going to like. Usually because it has to do with me doing or saying something wrong.

"Traditional mafia wives don't leave the bedroom with an unkempt appearance."

I'm not relieved by her pretty innocuous statement. I've known this woman intimately for most of my adult life. That look says her words are just the tip of an iceberg I'm about to go aground on.

"We both know that while you are an exemplary wife, in the ways that matter to you and me, you are not traditional." I've never wanted her to be a carbon copy of my mother and sure as hell didn't want my wife emulating *her* cold fish of a mother.

She nods her head in agreement. "We have always broken from tradition when it's important."

"Yes."

"If our nephew's almost fiancée wants us to call her Candi, that's what we call her. We do not disrespect other people for the sake of tradition or what is considered appropriate by some."

"You know I call her Candi." That doesn't mean I understand why she eschews the use of her given name.

One far more acceptable for the wife of a man as high up in the mafia as Angelo.

"I am aware, Sal, but you do it under duress."

"Only you know that," I say defensively.

"I would think that I'm the one that matters most." My beautiful wife sighs. "I am also struggling to understand why you are so against the relationship."

"Angelo could have married a woman that would shore up Severu's support in Chicago or New England. After what the Sicilian godfather tried to pull, we need stronger bonds among the American Cosa Nostra." It's time we were more proactive about marriages happening between the different mafia territories.

Leaving behind so many of the old ways in a single generation might have been a mistake.

Ilaria's eyes narrow. "Angelo is already more than a decade older than you were when you and I married for the sake of the mafia. You know Enzo recommended more than one marriage to him and he refused every time."

"If Enzo had ordered him to marry, he would have." My brother could be harsh, but even with his own sons, he never demanded agreement to an arranged marriage.

He even made sure his daughter liked her future husband before he agreed to the marriage alliance with the Vegas Cosa Nostra.

"Yes, he would have. But then he and his wife would have been miserable. Or she would have been." Ilaria turns back to the mirror to put on her jewelry. "It's clear Angelo doesn't lack all emotion. Candi is proof of that, but he definitely doesn't share your passionate nature."

And my wife would pity a woman trapped in a passionless marriage. She's said so before and used it as her excuse for not encouraging either of our children to offer themselves to an alliance marriage.

At least Ilaria still believes she got lucky when she got me as a husband in *her* arranged marriage.

I lift her perfectly styled hair away from her neck and kiss her nape. "I'm happy to give you another example of that passion now."

We're in our fifties, but my desire for my wife still burns bright and hot.

Ilaria shivers and smiles at me in the mirror. "As tempting as that offer is, we are supposed to join Bianca and Salvatore for dinner tonight and if you want your son to believe you accept his wife, cancelling time with them is not the way to go about it."

"You are right, as always, *cara mia*." I kiss her nape again and step back. "When do you think they'll give us grandchildren?"

"Whenever it is, I'm sure we'll be two of the first people to know." Ilaria turns away from the mirror and meets my eyes directly. "Until then, we're not going to say a word about it to them, are we?"

"Of course not." I'll never forget how hard those kinds of questions were on Ilaria after we lost our first baby. "But I would like to have a grandson before I am too old to teach him the things a grandfather in *la famiglia* should."

"You mean like how to shoot a gun?" Ilaria teases. "I'm sure that's something Salvatore can teach his child, whether it be a boy or a girl, just fine like you did both him and Nerissa."

But will my son teach his children about duty to the Cosa Nostra? It's not Bianca being a former stripper that makes it hard for me to accept her as my daughter-in-law. It's the fact she grew up learning about the ugly side of the mafia so she doesn't have the innate loyalty to *la famiglia* women like Ilaria do.

But it's not Bianca on my mind when I speak next. It's our daughter, Nerissa.

"She wants to bring that boy to Christmas." Hands down, that's what really has me so fucking pissed off. My baby girl wants to bring a date to Christmas dinner. "You know what that means."

"First, he is a man, a made man no less. He is not a boy. And Nerissa loves him."

"She's the daughter of a consigliere. She can do much better than a soldier on a capo's crew."

"Ernesto isn't merely a foot soldier, and you know it. He's Domenico's second." My wife slips into her heels, increasing her diminutive height by a sensible two inches.

"With no hope of becoming capo himself one day."

Ilaria shrugs. "So? What's the real problem here, Sal? After all your talk about making an advantageous marriage, did you really think Nerissa was going to stay single forever?"

"Of course not. I know my beautiful, talented and intelligent daughter will marry one day. But she can do much better than Ernesto. She should be marrying a capo. Or at least the son of a capo."

Ilaria bursts into genuine laughter. "Can you see any capo in the Five Families allowing his wife to be second to another capo?"

"No, but once she's married, Nerissa will give up being her brothers second." And I'll be able to sleep better at night knowing she's not working on the front lines any longer

Ilaria stops in the act of putting away her makeup. She never leaves a mess behind her. Every room in our two homes, except her ceramics studio, stays immaculate. And it's not solely because we have excellent cleaning staff.

Her gaze fixes on me and it's not friendly.

No question, I have just fucked up royally even if I don't know what I said that was wrong.

She points at me like she's ordering my execution. "Listen to me, Sal De Luca. Our daughter is more than a satellite for some man's life. She is the center of her own universe. She's bright and beautiful and she's fierce as any woman I have ever known. Do you really want her to subsume her personal ambition for her husband's consequence?"

There is only one right answer that question. "No."

Ilaria nods, like she expected nothing less from me. "You know, I had a hard time with her getting made. But it was the path she wanted to take. And I'm very proud of the woman she has become.'

"You never treated her differently after she took her vow as a Cosa Nostra soldier like you did Salvatore." It's something I've never understood and one of the few things Ilaria and I have never talked about.

"He killed the woman he loved. That he could do that devastated my heart. And that you could ask him to do it made me realize that had I ever been the one to betray *la famiglia*, you would have killed me too."

"Never!" I would never hurt this woman. If she betrayed the family, which I can't even wrap my mind around as a possibility, I would take her on the fucking run.

"Really? Bianca once asked me why I was so upset with Salvatore, but not the man who ordered the hit. And the truth is, Sal, I was afraid that if I let myself think about the fact you ordered our son to kill the woman he loved, I didn't know if my love for you would have survived."

"Are you saying you don't love me anymore?" Something in my chest cracks open and pain like I have never experienced explodes inside of me.

Does this explain the way she has pulled away from me? Did Bianca's question force Ilaria to face the monster inside me and find him irredeemable?

My wife's face softens, but the sadness reflected deep in her eyes does not go away. "No, that's not what I'm saying. Watching Bianca with Salvatore has helped me to see that we love the men we love, for who they are."

"Does that mean you forgive Salvatore?" *Do you forgive me?* I silently add.

"If our son had loved Monica like he loves Bianca, he would have gotten them new identities and taken her on the run. Like you would have done if it had been me."

Relief squeezes my heart so tight, it feels like I'm having a coronary. "Yes, I would."

She nods. "Even so, what did it do to our son to be the instrument of that death? He's never been the same, though I see glimmers of the boy I raised in the man married to Bianca. If for no other reason, that would make me love her."

"I thought killing Monica would help Salvatore get over the shame of being duped by a woman." If I had it to do over again, I would have killed her myself.

My wife looks at me first with shock and then with pity. "That's such a masculine way of looking at things, Sal, but that's not how the heart works. I'm just glad that Bianca brought healing to Salvatore. She can bring healing to our family if we let her."

"I didn't know our family was broken." But Bianca has helped Ilaria to accept Salvatore's past and my role in it. "She's a special woman and I'll make sure she knows I think so."

If I learned anything from the shock of discovering my brother had been a closet artist and seeing how his paintings reflected emotions he never spoke about and how that impacted his entire family, it's that the words should be said.

Ilaria smiles approval at me, no shadow in her beautiful eyes this time. "Remember our first Christmas together, *marito*?"

HE GOT SNIPPED?!

I LARIA

I told Sal, the love of my life, to remember our first Christmas.

It was the moment I knew that the man I had married because of a mafia arrangement loved me like I had come to love him.

The first Christmas we spent together wasn't the first Christmas we were married though. No, that first Christmas he was away on business for my father. It was the last time I spent the holiday alone with my family and not the De Lucas.

Sal didn't even remember to get me a Christmas gift before he left. Or so I thought. I cried for three days after Christmas. But when he got back, I had the façade of the mafia wife fully back in place and the sentimental present I'd gotten him was tucked in the back of my sweater drawer.

He hadn't forgotten to get me a gift, but had wanted to wait to give it to me until we were together. It wasn't the last time my Sal misread the emotional impact of his actions.

After I opened, not one, but several gifts of lingerie and jewelry from Sal, I gave him the letter from the doctor saying I was pregnant.

Over the moon, he barely noticed the onyx and diamond cufflinks that matched the engraved ring in my sweater drawer.

That, I wasn't ready to give him.

Especially when not a single one of his gifts were personal to me. I wear jewelry as part of my armor, but don't care about it otherwise. And lingerie is about our sex life, not our love life.

At least, that's how I saw it back then.

No way was I giving him a ring engraved with the words, *sempre il mio amore*.

Always my love.

I'd fallen in love with my husband, the one thing my mother said I should never do. But Sal wasn't and still isn't anything like my father. My heart was safe in his hands, even if I didn't believe it that first Christmas without him.

Neither of us had used the L-word in those first six months of marriage, but I'd believed we both felt it. Then I was sure that he didn't.

I didn't learn how wrong until the following Christmas.

33 Years Ago

"So when can we expect a grandchild?" My father's voice carries across the Christmas dinner table and my stomach tightens to the point of pain.

"Yes, isn't it time you got pregnant again?" my mother asks.

As if the end of my last pregnancy was some kind blip on the calendar and not the devastating reality and traumatic event that it was.

Don Matteo looks at me. "How are you doing?"

That he shows more concern for *my* wellbeing than either of my parents is not lost on me.

I don't know how to answer. I'm eight weeks pregnant and scared, but that's not something I'm announcing right here, right now.

I haven't even told Sal yet. We didn't plan this. We were going to wait. And I'm not about to tell him the news or share my fears in front of our entire family.

It's been a very difficult year. After we lost our first baby late in my second trimester, I nearly died. The doctor was very clear that any future pregnancy I have would be high risk.

Sal was extremely attentive the three weeks I was in the hospital. When I came home, he spoiled me rotten and was so very careful with me.

I had to seduce him the first time we made love. That's not usually the way things go between us. But we both enjoyed it and I've taken the initiative several times since. Not that Sal let me stay in charge for long.

That's the way we both like it.

But that first time bore fruit even though he used condoms and has every time since.

Sal's mother smiles understandingly. "There's no rush. You're still very young."

"Nonsense. She's had plenty of time to recover from what happened in the fall," my father dismisses. "Look at Aria, she's already given Enzo two heirs."

Don Matteo frowns and my paragon of a sister-in-law makes a sound of distress. She has no idea about the jealousy that plagues me at how easily she fulfilled her purpose of giving heirs to the family.

Enzo shares a measured look with his brother before giving Sal a barely perceptible nod.

Sal's hand settles on my thigh. It's such an uncommon public display of affection I have to stifle a gasp of shock.

"You'll get a grandchild after we find an acceptable surrogate." My husband's announcement sends a shockwave around the table that rolls right through me.

I whip my head to the side so I can see his face. His jaw like granite, Sal is staring my father down. Papà's shock palpable, his mouth is agape, but no sound comes out of it.

"But you can't." My mother is never lost for words. "The contract stipulates a child with both DeLuca and Benetti blood."

"Invitro fertilization allows your daughter's ovum fertilized with my sperm to be inserted into a surrogate's uterus," Sal explains, his tone as clinical as his words.

But there's nothing clinical about my reaction.

Sal wants to use IVF to protect me even though he had to know our families wouldn't be happy about it.

"It's perfectly safe. There have been thousands of IVF babies born since the first one in 1982," Enzo states firmly.

"No grandchild of mine is going to be born out of a test tube." Papà slams his hand down on the table for emphasis making the China and cutlery rattle.

Sal doesn't so much as blink in the face of my father's fury. "Our baby will be born just like any other one."

Papà surges to his feet. "This is a breach of our contract. Don't expect to take over for me if you try to fob some other woman's baby off on us."

"I've harvested my sperm already and had a vasectomy," Sal says calmly. "IVF is the only way you'll be getting a grandchild out of your daughter and me."

"You son-of-a-bitch," my father roars. "I'll get her an annulment and marry her to a real man."

"Over my dead body." Sal's hand moves from my thigh and slides toward the gun he wears under his suit jacket.

Absolutely reeling from my husband's last claim, I blurt out, "I'm already pregnant."

Sal's body jerks like I delivered a blow. Does he think I've cheated on him?

"We knew it was possible, that's why you got snipped," Enzo says to his brother, proving the next Don of the Genovese was aware of Sal's plans.

"When?" I ask. "When did you get..."

Sal doesn't look away from my father. "Six weeks ago when you thought I was out of town on business. I got the all clear a couple of days ago. I was going to surprise you tonight."

His implication has to be obvious to everyone at the table. Sal planned to have sex without condoms.

"That is not appropriate conversation for the Christmas dinner table." My mother-in-law's tone brooks no argument.

"That's alright then." My father sits down, like he hadn't just threatened to tear my marriage apart and give me to someone else like I'm nothing more than an interchangeable piece on his chessboard.

Again.

But all I'm thinking about is my husband getting a vasectomy to protect me from the risks another pregnancy would bring. That's just not something mafia men do.

I've never heard of a single one getting "the snip" as Enzo said.

"You'll have to get the vasectomy reversed, of course. One child is not enough to guarantee a successor for the capoship," my father says complacently. "Your concern for Ilaria's health is laudable, but you'll see. She'll handle this pregnancy just fine."

Another hand hits the table hard enough to make the China clink. But it's not Sal's.

"Enough!" Don Matteo roars. "If you attempt to meddle in my son's marriage again, or threaten to steal his wife from him, I'll make *your* wife a widow and piss on your grave."

Don Matteo was the money man before he became a leader in the Five Families, but you couldn't tell that by me. He's as scary as the old Don of the Genovese ever was.

"Are those new earrings a Christmas gift?" my mother asks my mother-in-law in a clear attempt to change the subject.

But Don Matteo keeps his gaze locked on my father until papà dips his head in obedience.

The Present

That first Christmas together I learned my husband loved me, though Sal didn't say the words until years later.

In so many ways, he is a product of his time, but in the important ones, he has gone his own way.

Maybe that's something *I* needed to remember.

FOREPLAY? THAT'S SPARRING.

N ERISSA

The pop of gunfire echoes through the concrete space under my family's building. Well, technically Salvatore owns the multistory apartment building, but my parents have an apartment for when they want to stay in the City and my apartment is on the floor below theirs.

An apartment I now share with Nesto, not that anyone in my family knows that little tidbit of truth.

The target ranges is part of the gym complex Salvatore installed after taking ownership of the building.

My Glock kicks, steady and controlled, as I unload the last round into the center mass of the target.

Nesto, arms crossed and leaning against the wall, watches me with the infuriating calm of a man who already knows how this is going to go.

"Nice grouping," he says, pushing off the wall. "Little high on that last one. You compensating for something?"

I smirk and eject the clip with a sharp click. "You'd know if I were."

He walks toward me slowly, like a predator approaching his mate, not prey. "I do know. Which is why I'm wondering why you're showing off."

"Maybe I wanted to remind you I can shoot just as well as you."

"*Better* than me, maybe, *cara mia*?" His eyebrow lifts, mocking.

"I didn't say that." I turn, slide a fresh clip in, and chamber a round with one hand. "But if the holster fits..."

He steps into my space, eyes locked on mine. "Careful. That confidence is gonna get you pinned."

"Promises, promises."

Before I can blink, he's spun me around, pressing me back against the padded mat wall, his thigh between mine, hands braced beside my head.

"Still cocky?" he growls, voice a gravel-paved threat against my ear.

"Always." I tilt my chin up and grin. "But you like that about me."

"I like a lot of things about you." He grinds his hips against me just enough to make his point.

I hook my leg behind his and flip us with a move I perfected sparring with my brother, who I so do not want think about right now.

Now Nesto's the one against the wall, breath catching as I press my body to his.

"I like winning." I brush my lips over his.

He grabs my hips and flips us again.

Now I'm back against the wall, laughing and breathless as he kisses me like he means to own the next decade of my life. Maybe longer.

And when he finally pulls back, he murmurs against my lips, "Call it a draw?"

I wrap my arms around his neck. "Only if we settle it upstairs."

His grin is pure sin. "Race you."

We're both vibrating in the elevator on the way up to our floor.

I barely get the door closed before he has me against it, hands greedy, mouth demanding. He tastes like sweat, competition, and the kind of lust that doesn't fade with time—it builds.

"You flipped me," he growls, kissing down my jaw. "You *really* flipped me."

"Didn't see that coming?" I breathe, arching against him as he palms my breast through my tank top.

"Oh, I saw it," he mutters, voice gravel, hands under my shirt now. "I let it happen."

"Liar."

His laugh rumbles in his chest, low and wicked. "Doesn't matter. You want the win?"

I nod, breath hitching.

"Then get on the bed and keep your hands to yourself."

My thighs clench. My mouth dries.

"Yes, sir."

He stills.

His eyes burn into mine.

"Say that again."

I walk slowly, deliberately toward the bed, pull off my shirt, then turn and meet his gaze with a wicked grin. "Yes, sir."

"Fuck." The word's a promise as he stalks toward me.

He peels off his shirt with one hand, throws it to the floor. Pants follow. The sight of him dark-eyed, built, and feral as hell is enough to make me forget how to breathe.

He pushes me back onto the mattress, kneeling between my legs like he's about to pray. Or sin.

"Hands on the headboard," he commands. "You move, it's over."

"You wouldn't."

"Try me."

I do as he says.

He kisses a path up my inner thigh, hands anchoring my hips while his mouth takes me apart—lick by wicked lick—until I'm gasping his name and begging for more. And I *never* beg.

He rises over me, sliding inside with a punishing thrust that knocks the breath out of me.

My hands strain against the headboard.

"Good girl," he rasps, moving deep and slow, grinding against the spot that makes me see stars. "So fucking good for me."

"Yes," I choke out, hips rocking instinctively. "Harder."

"No. You wait for it." He bites my shoulder—not to hurt. To let me know who's in control. "I'm in control now."

And I love it.

Love giving it to him.

Love the way he handles me like I'm both his treasure and his challenge.

Love that when I *do* fall apart, it's because he *made* me. Controlled my pleasure every second of the journey. Loved me in a way that's every bit as ruthless as the world we live in and utterly perfect for me.

I come screaming his name, feeling his sex swell inside me and flood me with his heat as I do.

Afterward, he's flat on his back, chest rising and falling, one arm draped behind his head like he *didn't* just rearrange my entire soul.

I'm curled beside him, leg tossed over his hips, cheek on his shoulder.

He hasn't said a word since we came down. Just that smug Sicilian smirk pulling at the corner of his mouth.

Typical.

"You good?" he finally murmurs, voice rough from effort and maybe...pride.

"More than." I stretch like a cat, thoroughly satisfied. "You're not bad at that. Should've been a full-time profession."

"Smartass."

"You love it."

"I tolerate it." He turns his head just enough to kiss my hair. "Barely."

I grin. And then, in my sweetest, most innocent voice: "Yes, sir."

He tenses.

Oh, that got him.

His hand slides from my hip to my ass, a slow squeeze that's equal parts warning and promise. "You keep calling me that, *cara mia*, and you'll be tied to this bed before sunset."

I hum. I see no downside to that. "Kinky."

"Nerissa."

I lift my head to look at him, all wide eyes and fake innocence. "Yes, *sir?*"

His eyes darken. "One more time. I dare you."

I trail a finger down his chest, circling his abs with deliberate slowness. "Yessir."

He grabs my wrist and flips me beneath him in one fluid movement, pressing his full weight into me, his cock already stirring again against my thigh.

"You really don't know how to stop when you're ahead, do you?"

I grin up at him, smug. "But where's the fun in that?"

He groans, lips finding mine. "Round two it is."

And if I lose again?

Well, this is the one and only place I'll enjoy the hell of not being the victor, because in losing my control to him I always win.

YOU WANNA DATE MY DAUGHTER?

S AL

The hospital is under heavy guard for Catalina's labor. Our soldiers patrol the halls with double the security and zero access except to immediate family and Catalina's medical team on this floor.

There are snipers on the roof and a soldier with a rocket launcher to take out any unidentified helicopters.

I'm not sure how my nephew will circumvent accusations of terrorism if it gets used, but knowing Severu, he's got a plan in place.

Every single person in the hospital has been vetted, and those we couldn't verify have been moved to one of the mafia run clinics. No new patients will be taken in while Catalina is here either.

Severu is taking no chances with the safety of his wife and soon-to-be-born son.

The rest of the hospital is locked down like a military compound, but when I open the door to Catalina's suite, the air is filled with joyous expectation.

Severu is not out here with the rest of the family, but that is no surprise.

He will be at Catalina's side during the entire labor and delivery, and I doubt he will leave until he can take her and their baby home. I was the same with Ilaria when she gave birth to Salvatore.

Not that I had snipers on the roof or anything so elaborate. Nor did his father when Aria gave birth to him or Miceli. But Severu is a different man than any of us.

In some ways he is more ruthless and others more vulnerable to the emotions that he holds for his family.

Ilaria looks up and her smile, as beautiful as it was on at our wedding, is more unguarded than that day 34 years ago.

Having gone through what we did, she'll never pester our son and daughter-in-law about giving her grandchildren, but she's thrilled to become a great aunt again.

I return her smile and walk toward her as my phone rings. The ringtone indicates it's one of the capos.

I put my finger up and her eyes dim a little as I answer. "Go."

"Big Sal? It's Stefano. We've got a problem with one of our longtime clients refusing to continue paying tithe."

"Who?"

He says a name and I know why he called. The business owner is an old friend of Stefano's and the capo doesn't want to come down heavy on him. But if I give the order, he can abdicate responsibility.

"Why are you calling me?" I demand, even though I know.

"I don't want to bother Miceli with it."

In other words, he's aware that Miceli is still pissed at him for the way Stefano treated his daughter. Candi.

Fuck, no wonder she doesn't want to use the name Kathleen. That was Stefano's mother's name.

"Why are you calling anyone? Do your f—" I stop the word that wants to come out of my mouth. "Do your job. If he wants to be exempted from our protection, then he knows what he has to do."

Move out of the building we own and that we control the rent on for the businesses housed there. Deal with the gangs and other syndicates on his own behalf and end up paying one of them a higher rate for a lot less protection. Get financing for expansion without our endorsement.

The list goes on.

Businesses pay us protection and it's not cheap, but it's not a one-way street. We give value for the tithe we expect them to skim off the top of their earnings.

"But he's been loyal so many years. Maybe we could renegotiate his terms."

Spinning on my heel, I storm out into the hall. "Did you just fucking say that to me?" I demand when I'm out of earshot of my wife.

Stefano blusters but I'm not in the mood.

The sadness Ilaria instantly hid as I turned away hits harder than it ever has. I brag she's the perfect mafia wife, but the truth is, she the perfect wife for me. Period.

No qualifiers.

Am I the perfect husband? Not so much.

But this old dog *can* learn new tricks.

"Come, on Big Sal," Stefano says like he's talking to an old friend. "You know Enzo always said to reward loyalty."

We've known each other for years, but friends we are not.

"Unless my brother has come back from the fucking dead and if he did, you wouldn't be his first visit, Miceli is your don, Bianchi. Do your fucking job or retire."

The man is still blustering when I hang up on him.

Turning my phone to silent so it will vibrate only, I slip it into my pocket. Any real emergency will hit Miceli first. I'm his advisor, not his underboss.

When I come back into the room, my wife, still as beautiful as the day we got married, remains seated in an armchair chatting with Aria, Bianca and Nerissa.

I'm sure the other women in the family's inner circle will show up soon enough.

Like she can feel my presence, Ilaria raises her head and her blue gaze meets mine.

There's a question in hers. *Are you leaving?*

I shake my head.

Her smile returns. "You made it, *marito mio.*"

"This is her first baby. I could have come ten hours from now and still made it for the birth," I joke, but my chest is tight from Ilaria calling me her husband like that again.

She's been doing it more the past few days and whatever changed between us, I don't want to go back to living at a distance from the woman I love.

"God forbid!" Miceli exclaims fervently. "Sev's on the verge of killing someone and Catalina has only been in labor for three hours."

If only he knew, but I don't repeat my prediction. Maybe the baby will come quickly. If it doesn't, I wouldn't put it past my oldest nephew to demand Catalina have a C-section.

Severu wanted her to consider it because of her hip replacement, but her OB told her a vaginal delivery would be safe. The woman is only still breathing because it would have upset Catalina to change doctors.

I know this because my nephew has grumbled those very words several times over the last months.

"He's every bit as bad as you were," Ilaria says with a private smile just for me.

I was a pain in the ass in the delivery room. I wonder what Severu is acting like right now? If he's like me, he's demanding pain meds and ice chips for his wife.

We share a moment remembering the birth of our son. I watched Ilaria like a hawk her whole pregnancy and insisted on weekly visits with the OB from the beginning.

My nephews don't know how lucky they are that there are so many female doctors today.

Back then I had to suffer through watching another man touch my wife every appointment.

When her doctor put her on bedrest, I switched to working from the office in the penthouse to make sure she followed his instructions. I gave her our mansion on Long Island to celebrate the birth of our son.

After we adopted Nerissa, I bought Ilaria a vacation home in Martha's Vinyard. Every time we go, I have business to conduct with the Boston Cosa Nostra. The last two times I went, Ilaria didn't want to go with me, telling me that if she was going to spend time alone, she'd rather do it at home.

I didn't take the hint for a lot of reasons, but mostly because working is how I dealt with the grief of losing my brother. But I'm damn well not going to lose my wife to my own neglect.

My head is firmly out of my ass.

"Hey, pops." Salvatore lays a hand on my shoulder.

I turn and greet him with a kiss on both cheeks.

"I found that African violet you wanted to give Bianca for Christmas. It will be delivered via private jet in three days." I keep my voice low so the women don't overhear.

I learned a long time ago that my wife can keep track of her own conversation and any others within hearing distance at the same time. I've never assumed since then that the other women in my family couldn't as well.

"Thanks." Salvatore casts a familiar glance filled with the same kind of love I have for his mother at Bianca.

Seated on the sofa with Nerissa, Bianca senses her husband's regard and looks his way, smiling at him.

"That right there, son, the way your wife smiles when she looks at you. It's worth everything. Don't be an ass like me and ever take it for granted."

Salvatore coughs in shock. I'm not one for giving romantic advice. Hell, until recently, I wasn't a man who focused on the romance in my marriage at all, but I'm not giving up my wife's love.

This old dog will not only learn new tricks. He'll damn well master them.

Ilaria and I are lucky. Especially in this world. We still have each other. Look at Aria.

When Enzo died, I lost a brother, but she lost the man she loved with all her heart. Enzo and I, we were lucky bastards to marry the women we did. Women who could learn to love the men our father raised us to be.

Looking around me, I'm struck how different it was for us when Salvatore was born. Back then, luxury meant a birthing room with enough space to accommodate my mother and Aria. Both of whom wanted to be there to support Ilaria when she gave birth.

Her mother spent the day at the country club. Truth to tell, I don't remember much of my mother or sister's being there that day. I only know they were, but my focus was entirely on Ilaria, like it should have been in so many things.

I bet my beautiful wife remembers though.

This place has enough room for the whole family. As big as any upscale hotel suite, it's got two bedrooms, a full bathroom off the living area. There's another one in the "bedroom" kitted out as a birthing room complete with ultrasound machine and whirlpool for Catalina to use during labor.

"What's that look for?" Salvatore asks.

"I would never have allowed your mother to sit in a whirlpool during labor."

My son grimaces. "Bianca keeps reminding me that this is all state-of-the-art birthing shit, but I'm with you."

He drops his voice to a near whisper when he says shit and pride at the respect he shows the women in our family fills me. "You're a good man, son."

Salvatore's dark brows so like mine draw together. "Is something up? You're not sick and hiding it from mamma, are you?"

"Do you really think I could?" We both look over at Ilaria who turns her gaze to us with uncanny timing before lifting her own perfectly shaped brows in question.

I shake my head to tell her it's nothing, but she waits until Salvatore shakes his head too before looking away.

"Yeah, maybe not."

"She's proud of you too."

"I know. She treats me differently since Bianca came into our lives though." The tone of our son's voice makes it clear that by different, he means better.

"Your wife has helped Ilaria see both of us through different eyes." I hope my son can hear the gratitude I feel for that in my voice. "You couldn't have chosen a better woman to bring into our family."

Salvatore's eyes widen and then he looks at *me* with pride. "Thank you for saying that. Bianca still thinks you don't approve of her completely."

"I'm working on fixing that." And on that note, I walk over to greet the women.

First, I kiss my wife which makes her blush and I'm smiling when I turn and lean down to kiss my daughter's cheeks and then Bianca's before greeting my sister-in-law.

A month ago, I would have greeted Aria first to show respect for my brother's widow, but showing love for my daughter by marriage is even more important.

The ladies clearly expect me to join my son and nephew, but I've spent all day with made men. Now, I want to spend time with my wife.

When it becomes apparent to them I'm not leaving, Bianca offers to scoot toward Nerissa so I can join them on the sofa.

I smile. "Thank you, *cara*, but I've got a seat already."

She looks at me in confusion that turns to shock as I lift my wife up, take her seat and then sit her sideways on my lap.

"Sal! What are you doing?" Ilaria smacks my chest with the back of her hand, but she's laughing and that blush that always turns me on gets brighter.

The way she goes still tells me she can feel what she's doing to me.

Soon, my son and nephew join us, dragging over chairs from the dining table. When Ernesto arrives, they all play musical chairs so he can sit beside my daughter. Bianca stands and offers Ernesto her seat beside Nerissa.

He looks torn between being polite and refusing and his clear desire to be near my daughter. Bianca doesn't give him a choice, pushing him to sit down. My son makes a sound that causes the hair on the back of *my* neck to rise when she puts her hand against another man's chest.

Ernesto sits.

Aria rises from her chair, insisting someone else take her larger seat to save space like I'm doing with Ilaria. She sits down in one of the dining chairs, her expression serene, but we all know that look.

And it means she won't be moved from her choice.

After initially trying to get her to go back to her seat anyway, Miceli and Salvatore immediately start arguing over who gets the armchair.

It would be perfectly acceptable for one of them to tell Ernesto to move and take his spot, but neither do, accepting his place beside my daughter like I'm still struggling to do.

"Róise's not even here," Salvatore points out.

Miceli scowls. "She'll be here soon enough. Her last class ended thirty minutes ago."

I'm pretty sure my nephew is about to play the *don* card when Ilaria clears her throat. "Miceli, *caro*, call the concierge assigned to the suite and get two more settees brought in. They can remove the table and chairs to make space, and we can all be comfortable."

As long as my wife stays exactly where she is, I don't care about the seating arrangements. With no intention of offering my spot to my don, much less my son, my arms tighten around Ilaria's midsection.

She lays her hand over mine, lacing our fingers. This woman.

"They'll do that?" Bianca asks, her voice tinged with disbelief.

She still doesn't fully realize what it means to be a De Luca in New York.

"Of course, they will," my wife replies. "The Five Families funded this hospital and supply the majority of income that keeps it running."

"Wow. I mean I knew Salvatore had more say in my care than he should have, but I thought it was because of the mafia thing." Bianca makes air quotes when she says *mafia*. "Not because you all pay their wages."

Miceli, who had stepped away to follow my wife's suggestion returns, pocketing his phone. "It'll take an hour."

I don't ask why so long because if it could have been done faster, my nephew would have made it happen.

Salvatore doesn't ask either. Instead, he drags one of the remaining dining chairs over and places it right next to his own. Once again pride fills my chest at my son's behavior.

He is a capo, but his cousin is don and Salvatore shows respect for that distinction by leaving the armchair for Miceli and Róise.

Normal conversation resumes as we all wait for an update from the birthing room. My eyes aren't on the room full of family though. Not really. They're fixed on my daughter.

Even sitting there on that small sofa with her boyfriend, Nerissa owns her space, not as the consigliere's daughter. Not even as her brother's second-in-command, but as a made woman in her own right.

She's sharp today, dressed in tailored black slacks and a blood-red blouse, boots that are stylish but would allow her to fight if she needed to. Small gold hoops glint in her ears. I miss her afro, but long hair can be a hindrance in a life and death situation and she keeps hers cut close to her scalp.

Her tiny tight curls are beautiful though, as is my daughter. Inside and out.

She laughs, her smile genuine, not the tight-lipped, practiced one reserved for her public facing role as a capo's second.

The reason for her amusement? Ernesto Ferrari.

His posture is relaxed, but he's alert, watching her back even in a secure space. He's dressed down, no tie, sleeves rolled to the elbows, ink covering his forearms. I wouldn't be surprised if my daughter's name is there amidst the other art.

They're that serious.

Fuck. My little girl isn't the fourteen-year-old I rescued form the streets and brought home to Ilaria. She's not a little girl at all and isn't that truth a stiletto straight through my heart?

Even I have to admit that Domenico's second-in-command is a good man. He's damn good at his job too. He's been at the young capo's side since the beginning, laying the groundwork for the cyber intel gathering they do, taking our online money laundering business into a whole other realm.

I know he's smart. Loyal. Dangerous enough to keep his place in the chain of command.

But is he worthy of *her*?

She says something I can't hear, and Ernesto's mouth quirks. He answers in a low tone that makes her eyes flash, her head tilting with interest. She pushes his chest lightly with her hand, and he lets her.

Doesn't flinch. Doesn't smirk. Just waits her out, patient and unshakable.

She's fire. He's iron.

And in this moment, I realize they fit.

Not like I expected. Not like I would have chosen. But they *fit*.

Ilaria nudges my chest with her elbow. "They remind me of us," she whispers.

I grunt. "I didn't wear damn hoodies and build firewalls."

"No, you wore thousand-dollar suits and built a life I was afraid to believe in." Her eyes soften. "But I did believe. And so does she."

I look at my daughter again, this time not as a father measuring a man against impossible expectations, but as a consigliere who's seen soldiers rise, fall, and fail. Ernesto isn't going to do anything but rise. And on his own merits.

Just like my son. Despite the advantages my position could have given Salvatore, he proved himself time and again.

Nerissa's boyfriend isn't flashy; he's solid and more confident than a lot of men twice his age. He doesn't blink when Nerissa takes the lead. That matters more than connections or family legacy, to a woman determined to make her own mark in our world.

He respects her.

And that's everything.

Managgia la miseria. That really is everything.

DE LUCA DYSFUNCTION

E RNESTO

The waiting room is full of De Lucas. It's like being in the lion's den. If the lions wore designer suits, smelled like danger, and made you want to count your bullets twice.

I'm surprised when Bianca offers me her seat next to Nerissa. More because neither Miceli, nor Salvatore demand it for themselves. The De Lucas aren't your normal ruling family, but with a capo, a don, his consigliere and the fucking godfather in their ranks, no one can deny they have more power than any other family in the Cosa Nostra.

Ilaria De Luca, Nerissa's mother is sitting on Big Sal's lap. I've never seen the consigliere look so at peace.

Until his eyes land on me. Assessing.

I'm close to Nerissa, not because she needs me there, but because my formerly frozen soul demands I be where the temperature is highest.

She's fire. Anyone with eyes can see that. What they don't see is how precise that fire is. She doesn't burn without aim. She incinerates what needs to be destroyed and lights a path through the dark for the people she loves.

More at home discussing territory strategy than where to get the best cannoli, my woman is calm, cool, and lethal. And so fucking sexy, she takes my breath away.

The first time I saw her, it felt like someone shot me while I was wearing body armor. My chest hurt and it was hard to breathe. As soon as I found out who she was, a capo's daughter – this was before Big Sal was promoted to consigliere – I knew I didn't have a chance.

We might be equal in rank, but our families are nowhere near equal. My dad was a drunken, low level soldier and my mom doesn't even know I'm a member of the Cosa Nostra. After dad died, she moved to Savannah to live with her sister.

We call each other at Christmas and our birthdays. That's about it. For all intents and purposes, I'm the equivalent to an orphan as far as the Genovese Family is concerned.

That didn't stop Domenico from giving me a chance on his crew, but I never would have approached Nerissa.

Good thing for me that the woman with a vise like grip on my heart doesn't wait around for a man to make his move. She came for me and none of my training in the military, or the mafia prepared me for her kind of assault.

Strength, honesty and a sensuality she never shows anyone but me is apparently my kryptonite. Even knowing that Big Sal would never approve of our relationship, I let myself get drawn into her orbit.

Now I'm completely addicted to my sun and if I ever lose her, it won't just be my soul that will go back to the frozen wasteland.

A weaker woman would leave me broken hearted. Nerissa De Luca stands up for what she wants and that's me.

I've served under two capos, worked with hackers, runners, lieutenants and killers. None of them scare me.

She does.

Not because I'm afraid she'll hurt me, but because I know I'd burn down my whole world if she asked me to.

I'd give up everything just to stay in her orbit.

And Sal De Luca knows it. His eyes are heavy on me. Measuring. Weighing. Judging whether I'm good enough to breathe the same air as his daughter.

I meet his gaze, mine steady.

I won't flinch.

I may not come from mafia royalty, but I'm the man who will take torture and a bullet before I let Nerissa fall. And I think—*I hope*—he knows that.

Nerissa brushes her hand against my forearm, the barest touch, but it singes me, marking me like a brand.

Big Sal notices, but instead of anger or disgust in his eyes, there's something else. Something I didn't think I would ever see directed at me from the consigliere.

It might actually be approval.

SAL

Róise arrives with the new furniture. Micelli greets her with a passionate kiss and then turns to the rest of us. "Stand up and move to the kitchenette area. This will go faster if we're all out of the way."

I don't know what the hell is going on, but I rise, holding my wife in my arms.

"Put me down, Sal. People are looking."

"Those people are family, *coure mio*." My heart.

Without this woman, I would not have one.

Eight of our soldiers file into the room, followed by the guards from the hall. Those men are part of Severu's personal security detail, the godfather, his wife and unborn child their priority.

I allow Ilaria to stand, tucking her against a wall, my body between hers and the rest of the room. Despite the soldiers being ours and trustworthy enough to be allowed into the suite where the godfather's wife is in labor, my caveman tendencies – as Ilaria used to teasingly call them – come into play.

Under the watchful eye of Severu's security, our soldiers remove all of the furniture in the room, including the sofa and armchairs. Then they bring in new pieces. The plastic wrapping around the unwieldy burdens explains the delay in their arrival. Every piece is new.

It takes less than twenty minutes for the soldiers to get rid of the shipping plastic and exit the suite.

When they are gone, there's a much smaller table with an upholstered bench seat on either side, five oversized chairs big enough for even men of our size to sit comfortably with our women in, and two elegant, wingback chairs that recline.

No doubt Miceli intends them for both his mother and Aria.

One of them will go unused. Unless Ilaria wants to risk the sturdiness of its structure with our combined weights.

"It will hold you both," Miceli says to me, his tone amused.

"The wingback? It looks delicate."

"It's not."

I nod, accepting his word. The oversized chair still looks more comfortable and that's where I lead Ilaria.

NERISSA

When the soldiers arrive with the furniture and my cousin orders all of us to stand up, I escape into the hall outside Catalina's birthing suite.

Ernesto follows, the tension in his body showing how alert to our surroundings he is allowing me to relax. He's the only man I feel this peace with.

I'm always on guard. Even with my dad and brothers. Not because I don't think they will protect me, but because I'm determined to prove they don't have to.

Two of my cousin's guards are still in the hallway, one at either end. Far enough away that if Ernesto and I keep our voices down, they won't be able to tell what we are saying.

There is no such thing as complete privacy for the member of a high ranking mafia family. And there's no higher ranking than mine. The De Lucas.

Sometimes, I still can't believe I'm part of it.

When I lost my first family, I thought I would always be alone. Especially after I had to run from the blood family I'd been sent to live with after my parent's death.

Then dad found me sleeping in alleyway, scavenging for food and using my fists on anyone who got close enough to try to touch me. I didn't trust him at first, but he proved he wasn't like the others.

He wanted to help me.

And then I met mamma. She had a hole in her heart I recognized, because I had one too. It wasn't until after I graduated high school that I learned what had caused her grief.

She'd lost a baby before Salvatore and after him, the doctors were adamant that she couldn't risk another pregnancy. But she wanted more children.

Adoptions was out of the question while her father was alive. By the time he died and my dad took over as capo, mamma thought she was too old to have another child. And then dad brought me home.

I had a good life with my parents, but after their deaths, I'd known nothing but harm and fighting for my very survival. I was a housecat gone feral and mamma was the only one who could have gentled me into trusting again.

She's who I aspire to be. Like my birth mom, mamma resides in my soul like a guiding light.

Ernesto leans back against the wall, arms crossed, like he has all the time in the world, not rushing me to speak. No demand I pay attention to him.

He's a man complete within himself, but that doesn't mean he doesn't need me. He does. He says I'm his sun and I thrive in that role.

His current calm is trained nonchalance that masks how ready he is to spring into action. My man is controlled to the point of seeming emotionless. But he's proven he's not.

His emotions for the few he actually lets in run hot and fierce.

I'm one of those few. His boss, Domenico is another.

Their relationship is one of brotherhood. Ours is so much more.

It's everything.

And that terrifies me more than being in a shootout with three Colombians and no weapon but a jammed Glock.

"I needed air," I say, stepping up beside him. Like maybe he doesn't know.

He nods, digging in his pocket and then offers me a cherry Lifesaver.

When I was a little girl, there was always a roll of cherry Lifesavers in my stocking at Christmas. My dad would tell me to keep them around for when the world tasted sour, so I could remember there were sweet things too.

I stopped eating them after I ran away, convinced the world was nothing but sour. Even after I became part of the De Luca family, I didn't eat another cherry Lifesaver. Not until I told Ernesto the story about it.

Then he started keeping them on hand. And giving them to me when I need the grounding. Like now.

The world doesn't taste sour right now. Anything but. There is something so sweet happening in that birthing suite, it's making my heart hurt.

I take the lifesaver and lean my shoulder against his. "You doing okay?"

He huffs a laugh. "I'm standing in a hospital full of mafia royalty, waiting for a godfather's heir to be born, and trying not to imagine your father breaking my fingers for breathing wrong."

I pop the Lifesaver in my mouth, letting the burst of sweet cherry goodness explode across my tastebuds. "My dad likes you."

"He respects me. Not the same thing."

He's right. "He's coming around," I say softly. "And my mom thinks you're good for me."

"I've never seen your parents like that."

He doesn't mean affectionate, because my dad always greets mamma with a kiss and never leaves without doing the same. But her sitting on his lap? That's a new one, even for me. "Me either."

"They have something special."

"They do." For a while, I thought my dad lost sight of that.

I'm glad he pulled his own head out of his ass before me and Salvatore had to help him do it. With a hammer and a chisel.

Nesto turns toward me and pulls my body around so we're facing each other. "So do we."

"Yes."

"Something I never want to lose. Your dad could leave me bleeding on the pavement." Nesto's voice is filled with gravel. "I'd still choose you. Every time."

The air sucks right out of my lungs.

He's not dramatic. Not prone to speeches or sentiment. That makes this moment mean so much more.

I reach up, wrap my hand around the back of his neck, and pull his forehead to mine. "Choose me again tomorrow," I whisper. "And the day after. Because I'll be choosing you too."

His breath hitches.

And then his mouth brushes mine—slow, reverent, and achingly tender.

Not a kiss made for seduction. A vow.

When we break apart, his hand slides down my arm to take mine as if he'll never let go.

And I hope he never does.

SAL

I notice Nerissa and Ernesto are missing and after making sure Ilaria is ensconced in "our" chair, I say, "I'm going to check on our daughter."

She rolls her eyes.

My dignified, perfect mafia wife *rolls her eyes*.

I trace my finger down her cheek. "What?"

"Nerissa is an adult. You do realize this?"

Managing not to roll my own eyes, I nod. What the hell alternate universe am I in right now that I even have that urge?

Ilaria gives me a look that has been keeping me on my toes for over thirty years. "Be nice."

"I'm a Cosa Nostra consigliere." Leaning down, I kiss her and I take my time about it. I lift my head and speak against her lips. "There is nothing nice about me, *cuore mio*, and we both know that is the way you prefer it."

Her eyes are unfocused and her cheeks glow pink when I walk away.

Nerissa and Ernesto are across the hall, a few yard to the left of the door, completely lost in their own bubble.

My daughter leans her head against her boyfriends in a show of vulnerability so rare it takes my breath from my body.

He's holding her like she's the most precious thing in the world. No grabbing. No groping. Just a man steadying the center of his gravity.

And when she pulls him down to whisper something I can't hear, his face changes.

Softens.

Then he kisses her.

Not with hunger.

With *care.*

I should look away. It's a private moment, one I have no right to.

But I don't.

Because no matter what I've been telling myself, this is what I've been waiting for. Not to see how well he shoots, or how high he rises within *la famiglia.*

To see how he loves her.

I spent too many years measuring men by what they could do for the Genovese, but Ilaria has reminded me what really matters.

And that is how a man treats the woman he claims.

Ernesto reveres my daughter. I recognize the signs because anyone looking at me with Ilaria in a private moment would see them as well.

I've been caught up in finding *someone worthy* of my highly intelligent, beautifully ruthless daughter, but I've been using the wrong measuring stick. The only one that matters is the depth of Ernesto's love.

If I'm not misreading things, it's as deep as I could want it to be. Hell, he showed up today, didn't he?

Outsiders don't feel comfortable among us De Lucas. I have to admit, I'm part of the reason why. And entirely on purpose. But he's here for my daughter regardless.

That says a lot.

Leaving them without interrupting, I return to my wife who is right, as she has been so many times throughout our life together.

This time about what is best for our daughter.

It's late.

The hospital suite's lights are dim now, the bustle of family replaced with hushed conversations and quiet anticipation.

Catalina is still in labor, but the mood has shifted. The initial excitement muted to quiet anticipation of my great-nephew's birth.

Angelo and his girlfriend, Candi, arrived earlier with coffee, mulled cider and cookies baked by her mother and little sister. A sweet gesture, according to Ilaria.

So, not Angelo's idea, but the only woman in the world my nephew-by-choice will ever love. *Could* ever love, according to my wife. It looks like she's right again.

Ilaria and I shared mulled cider from a single mug, the rest of the family fading into the background as we reminisced about Salvatore's birth.

Now, she's asleep, her head resting against my chest.

Miceli, Salvatore, Bianca and Nerissa are playing cards at the table. Aria is asleep with her feet up in one of the wingback chairs.

Candi and Angelo are tucked together on one of the oversized chairs, whispering. If I didn't know better, I'd say my nephew-by-choice is looking broody. Brooding I'm used to, but he's got his hand on Candi's lower belly and look of longing on his face.

The Christmas proposal he's planning can't come soon enough if he's that keen to start a family.

Róise is curled up under a bright pink fleece throw, listening to an audiobook, but Ernesto stands alone, leaning against the wall by the card players.

Still on duty. Always watching.

Rising slowly, I'm careful not to disturb Ilaria. I cover her with my suit jacket like a blanket. She turns her head and inhales, snuggling down with a peaceful look on her beautiful face.

I'm tempted to stay right where I am, but it's time to settle some things.

Ernesto notices my approach immediately and meets my eyes. There's no worry in his, no fear. His nod of respect is welcome, so is his lack of anxiety.

My daughter cannot live her life with a man intimidated by her father. She needs strength to match her strength and it looks like she's found it.

I jerk my head toward the door. "I'm getting some coffee. Join me."

It's not a request and he doesn't take it as such. After leaning down to kiss Nerissa's temple, he follows me from the suite.

I wait to speak until we are downstairs in the nearly empty cafeteria. There's a skeleton crew in here this late at night, but the coffee is fresh and a chef's on duty.

Rather than get the espresso I planned, I reach for a bottle of water, knowing that would make Ilaria happy. She's all about keeping my heart healthy these days and wants me to limit my caffeine intake.

Ernesto gets coffee and joins me at a table by the windows. Oh, to be thirty-five again. Ilaria never got on me about eating steak back then.

There are a lot of benefits to being fifty-five though. Not least of which is more wisdom than I had twenty years ago.

I take a long swig from my bottle of water and put it down so I can pull a small velvet pouch from my coat pocket and hold it out.

No words. No preamble.

He looks at it, then at me.

A flicker of something crosses his face: surprise, maybe. Wariness. He takes the pouch and opens it.

Inside is a vintage gold tiepin. Simple. Elegant. Embossed with the De Luca crest.

It has been passed down in my family for over one hundred years. My father wore this tiepin the night he made his vow as the first De Luca to be Don of the Genovese. When our father passed, Enzo got the ring and I got the tiepin.

Both hold significant family history.

"Sir..." Ernesto's voice is low, steady. But I hear the edge. The question.

"It's been in our family since the first De Luca came from Sicily to New York. Enzo wore it the night he became don, so did my father. I wore it when I took my vow as capo. I leant it to my nephews when they took their vows as dons and when Severu took up the mantle of godfather. Salvatore wore it when he took his vow as a capo."

Understanding registers in Ernesto's gaze. He stares down at the pin like it's a weapon. Like it's a promise.

"You wear it when you ask her." My voice is rougher than I mean it to be.

"Thank you," he says quietly.

"She's everything." Our gazes locked, I let mine show how much I mean my words. "You treat her like it."

"Always."

I nod. That's enough.

Because I'm giving my daughter and this man my blessing, not my permission.

Not that he asked for it. And that's something else I can respect. Ernesto is fully aware that Nerissa is the only one he needs to convince. Because even if I refused my blessing, if she loves this man, she'll marry him.

Ilaria is right about that too. Our daughter is too strong to bow to any man's dictates for her life, even her father's.

As it should be, no matter what tradition in *la famiglia* says.

When we return to the suite, Ilaria is sleepy eyed, but awake. As soon as I walk into the room, her eyes latch onto mine. I nod at the question in hers and she gives me a drowsy smile.

Cupping her face when I reach her, I ask, "Why are you awake?"

If Catalina had given birth, the suite wouldn't be so quiet.

"You were gone." Ilaria yawns, covering her mouth with her hand.

"Now I am back."

Ilaria allows me to shift her so I'm back in the chair and she's curled against me. Brushing her back under my jacket, I whisper, "I leant Ernesto the tiepin."

"I knew you'd do the right thing." She leaves the eventually unsaid but we both know it's there.

"We're a family of hard heads but we get there in the end."

She pats my chest. "That's what matters."

Seconds later, she's asleep again and I'm filled with a contentment I never knew at thirty-five. How could I? Back then I was driven by ambition and duty.

It took Ilaria's gentleness and courage to bring my heart back to life.

Cuore mio is still somnolent and I'm dozy many hours later when Severu comes out to inform us that Enzo Matteo, future godfather, is a healthy seven pounds nine ounces with the lungs of a lion.

He does not stay to be congratulated, but returns immediately to his wife's side.

As it should be.

AND BABY MAKES...

C ATALINA

I've never been this exhausted and this in love at the same time.

Severu's asleep in the chair beside the bed—still dressed in yesterday's suit pants and undershirt, arms folded, head tipped back. Even in rest, he looks ready to kill anyone who so much as breathes too loud.

I cradle our son against my chest, skin to skin. He's warm. Perfect. Everything.

A soft knock at the door breaks the stillness. I whisper, "Come in."

Severu's Aunt Ilaria steps inside, carrying a pale blue gift bag with one hand, a small insulated thermos in the other. Her heels click against the polished floor—of course she wore heels to a hospital. Of course she looks immaculate.

Aria did too when she came in to meet her grandson.

These women and their heels. Severu never lifted his moratorium on me wearing them, even after I was completely healed from my hip surgery. And I don't mind one bit.

Ilaria's eyes are soft, rimmed with unshed tears.

"I brought you tea," she says.

"You didn't have to—"

"I did." She sets the thermos down and reaches into the bag. "And I brought you these."

She pulls out an ultra-soft, chartreuse robe and a pair of comfy slippers in the same color. The kind of bright pick me up you don't realize you need until someone hands it to you.

I brought a robe and slippers to the hospital. If I hadn't, Severu would have, but this gift...it's so me. A silent but heartfelt way of showing me that she supports and accepts me just as I am.

Just like Aria. These two women have done so much to make my life as the wife of a don and then godfather, not merely bearable, but wonderful.

"It's perfect," I say quietly.

"So are you." She winks and then her gaze lands on the baby. "Can I...?"

I nod. Ilaria sits on the edge of the bed and carefully, reverently, takes Enzo into her arms.

"He looks like Severu," she says after a long moment. "But I see you in him too. In the way he holds his mouth. In the stubborn set of his jaw."

I blink back tears.

"Thank you," I whisper.

She looks up. "For what?"

"For seeing me. For letting me in."

"I didn't let you in," she says gently. "You walked in like you belonged. And you did."

The door opens again. Big Sal steps in. He's already scowling. "Where's his cap? His head's going to get cold."

Ilaria rolls her eyes and hands him the baby. "He's warm enough. We're indoors. Let her breathe."

Sal holds the baby like he's been doing it all his life. Like he *never* stopped.

"Well?" I ask, biting my lip. "What do you think, consigliere?"

He looks down at the baby—so tiny in his massive hands—and something flickers in his expression. Not softness. Not quite. Something ancient and proud.

"He's perfect," Big Sal says gruffly. "Just like his mother."

"That's what I said." Ilaria leans into her husband's side.

He tucks her close and then smiles. "He'll be as stubborn as his father, though. God help us all."

I laugh. Ilaria does too. And for one shining moment, everything is exactly as it should be.

NERISSA

No one warned me that my cousin having a baby would turn me into a *disaster*.

I didn't get like this when Giulia had Neri. Of course, I didn't meet him until he was nearly a year old and I wasn't with Nesto then.

The possibility that this could one day be me, never even register. Now, it's all I can think about.

A family with Nesto, another baby to add to the De Luca legacy.

I step into the room with a wrapped gift balanced in one hand and a glare ready in the other. Because if anyone says I'm crying? They're getting throat-punched.

Catalina excepted of course.

Severu? Not so much. Godfather, or not.

A little voice in my head mocks me for my inner rant knowing I wouldn't disrespect the godfather, ever. He might be family, but he's more. The head of the Cosa Nostra in America, there's not a more powerful man in our world.

And I respect him more than I'll ever be willing to admit.

Catalina looks up from the bed, sleepy but radiant in the bright green robe mamma bought her. She gives me a tired smile and nods toward the bassinet beside her. "He's ready to meet his fiercest cousin."

"Damn right I am," I mutter, making my way over. "But don't tell Salvatore. He'll get butt hurt."

Catalina's smile is wan, but genuine.

Enzo is sleeping like a snug little burrito in a navy swaddle embroidered with tiny gold crowns and a large De Luca coat of arms in the center. This little guy is mafia royalty and just like any prince, his life is mapped before him.

But I know Severu and Catalina. They'll raise their little prince with love and the De Luca sense of honor.

"Hey there, *bambino*," I whisper, crouching over the bassinet. "I'm Nerissa. Your cousin. Grown men fear me, but you've already ruined me. Don't go getting a big head over it though."

His tiny mouth puckers and relaxes. My heart does something terrifying.

"Would you like to hold him?" Catalina asks, sitting up straighter.

I freeze. "What if I break him?"

"You took down a 250-pound enforcer last month," she deadpans. "You'll be fine."

I slide into the armchair beside the bed, and Catalina hands him to me like he's made of stardust and glass. He settles against my chest with a sigh.

That's it. I'm gone.

"Holy shit," I breathe. "I'd kill for this baby."

"You'd kill for most people in this room," Severu says from the doorway, smirking.

I don't deny it.

Dad walks in behind him. "Just don't teach him how to build a car bomb until he can walk."

"I was thinking more kindergarten," I say sweetly.

Catalina snorts. "That's what you think. You've got the biggest heart of all of us."

"I'm still not crying." I never cry outside of the bedroom. And that's different.

"Of course not," Severu says, and places a gentle hand on my shoulder. "You're Nerissa De Luca. Steel spine. Killer aim. Soft as hell where it counts."

I roll my eyes, but my voice cracks. "Don't make me prove it by gutting someone."

Baby Enzo makes a tiny noise in his sleep.

I lean down and whisper against his hair, "Don't worry, *cuginetto*. No one's ever going to so much as touch you. Not on my watch."

Nesto is waiting for me when I come out of the birthing room. Pushing away from the wall, he puts his hand out and I take it.

"Ready to go home?" he asks, his voice strangely gentle.

I nod.

"That'll be us someday," Nesto says, like he didn't just drop a nuclear bomb on the way to the elevator.

But my heart...well, it kind of wants those words to be true.

OOH LA LA SPICY SPICE

N ERISSA

It's only four in the afternoon, but I'm curled up in our bed with wet hair and wearing one of Nesto's t-shirts. Zero defenses.

He had to take a call from Domenico when we arrived, so I showered first. After two long days at the hospital, I'm wiped, but I want Nesto here with me before I fall asleep.

I always sleep better with his arms around me.

He walks into the room still in slacks and his undershirt, muscles rippling under the tight white cotton knit. My mouth goes dry and other parts get wet.

I tell my ovaries to settle down. Now is not the time. I need sleep. Not sexing up.

My ovaries ignore my good sense and keep telling the rest of my body, what we really need is him.

Nesto lifts a small velvet pouch like it's made of glass.

My heart crawls into my throat. "I've seen that pouch before."

Ernesto walks over and sits beside me on the bed. "Your father leant this to me."

I blink. "He did?"

That can only mean one thing.

Nesto nods once, then opens the pouch. The gold tie pin gleams in the late afternoon sunlight filtering in through the crack in the curtains.

My breath catches. "He...I..."

"I didn't ask for it. He just... offered." Nesto's voice is quiet, careful, like he's still wrapping his head around what happened.

I stare at the piece. It's not just jewelry. It's a piece of De Luca history. All the men in my family wore that pin when they took vows of leadership in the Cosa Nostra. I wore it the night I became Salvatore's second-in-command.

I reach for it, then stop. "Did he say what it was for?"

"He told me to wear it when I ask you." Nesto doesn't smile, but there's quiet joy in his tone.

Every breath in my body stills. I look at him. Really look.

This man. My lover. My safe place. My equal. My match.

And now... my future.

My throat tightens. "He trusts you."

"I think he does." Nesto sets the pouch down on the nightstand and cups my face with both hands. "I would've asked you without it. Or his approval."

"I know." My smile trembles. "But now you'll be asking with all the weight of the De Luca legacy behind you."

"Only thing I care about," he murmurs, brushing a kiss against my lips, "is having you say yes."

"I already have," I whisper. "Every damn day."

"Say it now. The word, Nerissa. I want the vow."

"Yes, Ernesto Ferrari, I will marry you."

The next kiss is filled with heat and dominance. "You belong to me."

"I have from the beginning."

Ernesto pins my wrists above my head with one large hand, his body covering mine like a promise and a threat.

His eyes burn with a fire only I ignite in him. "And I belong to you, to every last molecule of my DNA."

"Good thing because I have plans for that DNA." Plans I'm not ready to talk about yet, but someday sooner than later.

An animalist sound comes from low in his throat and he kisses me with bruising intensity.

Everyone thinks I'm the fierce one. The cold one. The one with the edge. They're not wrong.

I've killed men. Run negotiations that had the soldiers around me sweating. Carried the De Luca name on my back like a battle standard since the day I took my vow.

But here, in our bed, I'm just a woman.

His woman.

And I don't have to lead.

"You've been running on adrenaline for days," he murmurs. "I can feel it under your skin. Let me burn it out of you."

"Yes," I breathe. "Please."

I trust him to know what I need. And once again, he proves that he does, pulling the t-shirt off of me before pinning my hands back to the bed.

With reverence. With command.

He takes a beat just to look at me naked, taking in every inch of melanin rich skin, every curve and muscle I've forged into armor over the years.

The first time he did this, I squirmed and demanded he get on with it. He tied me to his bed and edged me for two hours before letting me come so hard, I nearly passed out.

There have been times since then that I did lose consciousness after an orgasm too strong for my body to bear.

Now his eyes on me trigger my muscles to loosen and my heart to quicken.

Because he sees me. *All* of me.

"You're so damn beautiful," he growls. "You always are. But like this? Breathless and soft for me? You wreck me."

Wanting to touch too, I tug at his hold on my wrists.

But he shakes his head. "Tonight, I'm the only one touching."

I suck in a fortifying breath. My body knows what that means, and it's not a quickie and sleep.

Nesto presses my hands to the bed. "Keep them there.'

He'll restrain me if I need it, but he prefers to command me with his body and voice alone.

When I nod my assent, he smiles. "Good girl."

Endorphins pour through me at those two words.

Then he touches me, fingertips feather light, drawing paths of goose-bumps along my sensitive skin. Down my arms. Over my stomach. Along my inner thighs.

I'm so slick I can feel my arousal running down to my ass and he hasn't even touched my pussy or breasts.

Finally, he skims his hands over my nipples and I moan. Already a shade darker than the rest of me, engorged with blood, they turn dark chestnut. Then and only then will he put his mouth on me there.

When, according to Nesto, they're too sweet to resist anymore.

He plays there for long moments, circling and touching until the hard peaks ache for his lips.

He knows. He always knows. "Look at those juicy nips just waiting for me to taste them."

Another gush of wetness adds to the moisture between my legs.

Nesto inhales deeply. "The smell of your desire makes my mouth water and my dick hard, and my good girl perfumes the air with it, don't you?"

"Yes," I breathe, feeling like my body's response to him is a gift only I can give.

Then his mouth is on one of my nipples, his tongue laving and his lips circling, but it's not enough and a low whine makes it past my lips unbidden.

Without warning, his teeth clamp down and his fingers pinch my other nipple to the point just this side of pain. My body bows in involuntary response, but I keep my hands pressed against the bed.

He keeps up the exquisite torture until I think I can't stand it anymore, but before I beg him to stop...or do it harder, his fingers unclamp from one nipple. He draws back with his mouth on the other, keeping it trapped lightly between his teeth until my breast is pulled up and away from my body.

Then, he opens his mouth and it falls back, sending a shudder through my entire body.

He goes back to the light touches and moisture pools in my eyes before spilling over to slide down my temples. Before Nesto, I did not cry. Not ever.

The way he takes care of me...the way he touches me, it makes the tears come and they are always a catharsis.

The torturously light touches continue until the tears stop and I feel hollow and whole at the same time. That's when Nesto lifts and bends first my left leg, and then my right one so I'm spread and displayed just for him.

He slaps my pussy. Pleasure vibrates from my clit to the rest of my body and I moan.

Nesto's smile is filled with warmth. With approval.

Then he lean down and with his face inches from my pussy, he slides two fingers inside me. There's no resistance from my soaked pussy.

"So wet for me already," he murmurs, mouth hot on my inner thigh. "You're hard as steel to the rest of the world, but your soft and drenched for me."

"Only for you," I whisper my agreement.

His fingers stroke slow, and measured, until I'm trembling. When he lowers his mouth and tastes me, I'm so on edge, I cry out.

My sounds spur him on. Nesto marks my most intimate flesh with pleasure. He alternates between sucking my labia and my clit, getting me hot and bothered with one until I'm on the brink, then shifting to the other, increasing or decreasing the pressure, whatever will keep me on the edge.

He doesn't stop. Doesn't relent until I'm crying out in wordless need.

Only then does he allow me to fall apart for him, utterly, beautifully undone.

There's no time to so much as bring my breathing back under control before he's over me, lining his big cock up to my entrance.

"Tell me who owns this," he growls against my lips.

"You do."

"And who do you belong to?"

"You." The word's barely a breath. "Only you."

He pushes inside me in one deep, powerful thrust. It's almost too much, but my body was made for this man and accommodates him like it does every time.

With soul stealing pleasure.

I moan into his mouth.

He takes me hard, steady, keeping my wrists pinned as he drives into me like he's claiming something he never intends to lose.

I surrender completely.

No power games.

No masks.

Just the raw, aching truth of us.

When we both shatter—his name on my lips, my name on his—it feels like something permanent carves itself into the fabric of the universe.

Us.

The water is warm, the scent of eucalyptus rising around us in lazy spirals of steam.

Ernesto sits behind me in the oversized tub, his arms curved around my body, his chest a solid wall against my back. I'm relaxed and heavy, floating in a place that's all skin and heartbeat and the safe silence that comes when nothing has to be said.

He brushes his hand up my arm, slow, like he's memorizing me again. "You good?"

"Mmm." My eyes don't open, but I add, "Better than good."

His nose nudges my temple. "Still here with me?"

"Always."

My voice is soft. Not because I'm tired, though I am, even more so than when we first got back from the hospital. But because I'm *allowed* to be soft here.

With him. In this space.

Nesto's fingers find mine and he twines them, connecting us. "You were fire earlier."

"You make me burn."

"No, *amate*, that's all you. My sun. My moon. My stars. My everything."

My heart in my throat, wanting to take a step back from the heaviness of the emotion between us, I try to tease. "That's poetic for a man who spent the last hour proving he has no mercy."

"I have none," he says simply, no laughter in his voice, not letting me hide here anymore than when our bodies are joined in deep intimacy. "Not when it comes to taking care of you."

A lump rises in my throat. I swallow it down with a breath, leaning back against his shoulder.

The faucet drips. The water laps gently at the sides of the tub.

And he just... holds me.

No demands. No expectations.

Only hands that glide over my skin with reverence. Only a kiss pressed to the top of my head like a benediction.

"You know," I say, after a long stretch of silence, "I never thought I'd find this."

He hums. "What's this?"

"A man who doesn't want me to be smaller. Softer. Quieter. Someone who sees what I carry and doesn't try to take it from me."

"I love you, Nerissa. Not some version of you that anyone else thinks should exist. *You*."

"I love you too, Nesto."

"I know, sweetheart, that's why we're getting married.'

Yes, that's why we're getting married.

No contracts. No plans or power grabs. Just a marriage of two people whose lives are better for having the other one in it.

ERNESTO

I wake to the scent of coffee which explains why Nerissa is not in the bed beside me.

Turning, I bury my face in her pillow and inhale her scent. My morning wood morphs from biological to turned on in a heartbeat. But Nerissa isn't here and I'm not about to jack off when the sexiest woman walking this earth is somewhere nearby.

I get up and pull on a pair of gray sweats. I have no idea why, but Nerissa replaced all my flannel pajama pants and black sweats with gray ones.

I don't care what color my sweats are or if I have pajama pants, or not. Mostly, around Nerissa, I prefer to be naked.

I find her in the kitchen. Barefoot in one of my white button-downs, sleeves rolled, hem brushing her thighs. Her skin glows against the fabric, dark and soft and perfect.

She turns, a beautiful smile on her face. "Coffee?"

"Yeah." I grab one of the pastries on a plate in the middle of the table. "When did you get these?"

More importantly, how did she get them? Nerissa is not dressed to go out, *or* receive deliveries.

"Delivery." She stirs a splash of cream into my coffee and hands me the mug.

Frowning, I take it, but I don't bring it to my lips. "You got a delivery? Dressed like that?"

"Relax, caveman. I had one of my crew leave it outside the door. No one got to ogle my legs."

"Good. I didn't want to have to start the day by blinding one of your brother's soldiers."

"They're my soldiers too."

"Just like all the soldiers working under me are mine too, but ultimately, they're Domenico's men."

"Does it bother you? Being an underboss?"

"Domenico doesn't structure his crew like that. There's no official second-in-command in the cyber division."

"But all the men know to come to you when Domenico isn't available."

"That's because I'm his favorite," I joke.

"It's because he trusts you implicitly like my brother trusts me." An old hurt flits across her face, but it doesn't stay there.

Salvatore and Nerissa argued over Bianca. My lover did not trust the other woman when she showed up in the capo's life out of nowhere. Nerissa naturally did a deep dive into Bianca's background. I helped her.

Unfortunately, what we came up with was not as it seemed and she nearly lost her job as Salvatore's second over her need to protect him from himself.

Bianca insisted on him reinstating Nerissa and is one of her closest friends now.

I'm proud of my girl for how she handled it all, but I damn near killed her brother for hurting her the way he did. I had already approached Domenico about taking my grievance to the don. I planned to ask for permission to confront the capo for his treatment of his sister based on family ties and her place in my life.

It would have been a physical confrontation because words were never going to cut it.

The audience with the don became unnecessary and Nerissa will never know how close I came to killing or maiming her third favorite man alive. I'm the first. And that still fucking blows my mind. Her dad's the second.

But she loves her brother with fierce loyalty that is only one of the reasons I love her.

"Eggs?" she asks, holding up a pan.

I shake my head, anticipation thrumming through my veins. Not for anything in particular. Just the anticipation of spending time with my woman.

She puts the pan down and saunters over to where I'm sitting. "What do you want then?"

Grabbing her wrist, I tug her down, but instead of sitting on my lap, she shifts so she's straddling it, the hot apex of her thighs pressed against my morning wood. She rocks a little and hums her approval.

I offer her a bite of my pastry and she takes it, not bothering to lick the icing from her lips after.

Leaning forward, I do it for her.

We go back and forth, feeding each other and taking sips of coffee from each other's mug. I don't know why it always tastes better when it's hers, but it does.

After feeding me most of another pastry and only letting me give her a couple of bites, Nerissa rests her forehead against mine. "I've never had someone take care of me like you do. You make me feel so safe, I forget I've got a knife under the pillow."

My lips quirk. "I noticed." I have to move the knife to the bedside table most nights.

Our lovemaking is too energetic to risk an accidental run in with her lethally sharp blades.

"I sleep better now." She pulls back and runs her fingers through my hair. "But you, you carry so much in silence. I see it. I feel it."

"Nerissa—"

"Nope." She kisses me again. "You gave me peace last night. Now I get to give it back."

So I let her.

She pushes my sweats down so my rigid cock springs upward and then grabs it and lowers herself down until the head is at the slick opening of her body. A shudder rolls through her and then she presses down further, rocking her hips until her tight, tight pussy fully envelops my cock.

She takes her time, not rushing either of us and when I come it's as profound as our two souls meshing. And that feels as right as anything ever has in my life.

The woman already owns my heart. She might as well have my soul too.

Afterward, she traces her initials on my chest with the tip of her finger. She doesn't say *I love you* like she did last night.

Not because it isn't true.

But because everything she does says it for her.

NERISSA

Dinner starts off like any other De Luca gathering which is to say, half the room is armed, the wine flows like water, and at least three people are pretending not to watch the exits.

It's Sunday. The Sunday before Christmas to be precise. Which means a family dinner. My parents, my brother and his wife, my cousins and their wives and now baby Enzo.

We're at Severu and Catalina's. It's not their turn to host, but mere days after Enzo's birth, none of us wanted Catalina to travel, even as far as Miceli and Róise's place.

The dining table is practically groaning from the pasta and meat dishes.

My leg jiggles and Nesto's hand presses down on my thigh under the table. Subtle, grounding.

I take a deep breath and then another. My heart settles and my need to move dissipates. Nesto squeezes my thigh and I look up from my plate.

He's asking me if I'm ready. I am, so I nod.

It's time.

I stand and clink my spoon against my glass. Nesto rises to stand beside me.

Conversations falter. Heads turn.

Dad leans back slowly in his chair, watching me with that unreadable stare that's been intimidating grown men since before I was born.

I lift my hand, the back to the rest of my family so everyone can see the ring.

The room gasps. That's the only way to explain it. Everyone makes a sound of shock. Everyone but my dad and mamma.

Aunt Aria clutches her chest. Cookie squeals. Candi launches herself out of her seat and practically tackles me with a hug. "Finally! I've been taking bets with the staff!"

Bianca lets out a soft, "Aw, *tesoro!*" and reaches for Salvatore's hand.

I look to Nesto, and joy shines out to me from the depths of his beautiful eyes.

And then... *Silence.*

The kind of silence that fills a room when everyone is waiting to hear what a dangerous man has to say. Which in this family is every one of them.

But it's dad we're all looking at as he sets down his wineglass and studies my beloved for a long, agonizing moment.

"You ask me for permission?"

Nesto's jaw tightens. "No, sir."

"Smart." Sal raises an eyebrow. "She'd have kicked both our asses if you did."

A beat.

Then dad lifts his glass to a chorus of laughter. "To the man my daughter chose...and the only one who could ever be worthy of her."

Miceli grins. "Hell just froze over."

Mamma wipes at her eyes, then lifts her own glass. "To love."

"To love," the room echoes.

Ernesto slides his arm around my back, pulling me tight to his side.

"This woman," he says, his voice deep and steady, "is the only reason I know who I am and where I'm going. I don't deserve her. But I'll spend the rest of my life proving I'm the man she deserves."

Someone says, "Swoon." I think it's Candi's mom, Mira.

A smile tickles at the corner of my mouth, but I agree one hundred percent. Nesto Ferrari is as swoony as swoony gets.

LA FUITINA

S AL

When Salvatore was little, he would wake us up before dawn on Christmas morning. After Nerissa became part of our family, Ilaria made it a point to wake our daughter that early with her stocking.

She said Nerissa deserved to know the magic of Christmas morning.

Now, it's just us and the sun hasn't broken the Eastern horizon, but I'm awake.

Ilaria's warm body is curved around me, her head pillowed on my chest. We used to sleep like this all the time, but as the years went on, we stopped.

Having her close like this is a privilege I will never take for granted again.

Grabbing the blue satin stocking from the bedside table where I left it late last night, I place it on top the covers where my wife will see it as soon as she opens her eyes. She doesn't wake for another hour and I enjoy every minute of holding her in the quiet.

"Mmm..." Ilaria rubs her cheek against my chest. "Such a nice way to wake up, hearing your heartbeat."

I instruct the lights to turn on at 50% through our smart speaker. As the room illuminates, Ilaria stops moving and then sits up with the eagerness of a child.

"You got me a stocking!"

"I get you one every year."

"But after Salvatore was old enough to know the difference, you put mine out with his on the fireplace."

"As you did mine." We'd stopped filling them with naughty things then too.

It wouldn't do for our son to see his mother pull a pair of silk lined handcuffs from her stocking, would it?

"I...yours is still hanging on the fireplace."

"Thank you. It's a good tradition."

She pulls her stocking to her and peeks in the top. "I like this one better."

The fuzzy socks that will keep her feet warm when she's reading in her favorite chair in the corner of our room are a bigger hit than the diamond earrings I gave her our first Christmas as man and wife.

I learned quickly that Ilaria isn't particularly fond of jewelry, wearing it like she does her designer clothes. As part of her uniform.

Next a small box of her favorite truffles from Switzerland comes out and she immediately pops one in her mouth before pulling out the small gift box.

Inside is a key.

"What's this for?" she asks.

"I sold the house in Martha's Vinyard."

Her eyes widen. "Why?"

"Because when we go on vacation together, there shouldn't be mafia business attached to it." Hell, I conducted business in Sicily when we were on our honeymoon.

I have a lot of missed opportunities to make up for and as a consigliere and not a capo, I can make the time to do that.

Tears sparkle in her beautiful eyes and she blinks them away. "What's the key to then?"

"A house on the coast of Portugal. There are no Cosa Nostra ties in Lisbon."

"You're taking me on vacation?" she asks, sounding shocked.

"Yes. For a month. We leave the day after New Years so you get all the holidays with the family, but then it's just us."

She drops the stocking and stares at me. "Just us? For a month?"

"No."

Before she can look too disappointed, I push her back onto the bed and pin her beneath me. "For the rest of our lives just us is my top priority."

"I love you, *marito mio*."

"And that makes me a very lucky man. You might have felt like embracing *La Fuitana*, but I'm so glad you went through with our wedding."

Ilaria looks confused and then her eyes warm. "If I'd run away, it would have been from the love of my life, I just didn't know it then. I'm glad I let my parents force me into marrying you too."

We both laugh a little at that, but I can only be grateful I never followed through on my plans to arrange a marriage for our daughter. She deserves the man of her dreams. I grateful with everything left of my tarnished soul that I turned out to be that man for the woman who makes my heart beat.

"I love you now and into eternity, Ilaria De Luca. Even death will not separate us. Our souls will wander the heavens together."

We're late for Christmas dinner with the family at Angelo's, but spending the morning in bed with my wife is worth it.

EPILOGUE 1: SANTO STEFANO

A RIA

The house smells like cinnamon, espresso, and Ilaria's lemon-glazed biscotti.

I love it here. I always have. It's a family home. Sal and Ilaria were always different from me and Enzo. I never realized how much until the last year.

Sal tells his wife he loves her. He has always told his children the same thing. Enzo loved our children. He loved me, but he kept his emotions on lockdown because he believed they were a weakness. Like his painting.

I wish I could have shared both with him in life. Maybe if we'd both allowed a little more humanity in, Enzo's heart wouldn't have given out like it did. Maybe if we'd have been as close as Ilaria and Sal, I would have noticed the signs of a man under too much stress.

There's no changing the past, but the future of our family is brighter than Catalina's smile when she looks at her son. And I can be part of making sure it stays that way.

Starting with embracing every bit of family joy this Saint Stephen's Day.

Strings of golden lights twinkle on the twelve-foot tree, and every wrapped gift is marked in calligraphy with color coded tags because that's what happens when your family includes a capo, a don, a consigliere, and a man who once alphabetized a hit list.

But this year, no one's looking at the gifts.

Because my youngest grandson is asleep in a plush bassinet well away from the tree, *and* the fireplace. Severu gives new meaning to the term *helicopter parent.*

Sophie is crawling across the floor, headed for the tree and Neri is chasing her ready to protect her from harm as if there's not a single adult in the room competent enough to watch out for his little sister.

I'm so happy Giulia and Raff chose to spend Christmas with us this year. Their lives are in Las Vegas, and that makes days like this ones to treasure.

"Someone take a picture of all that cuteness," Nerissa demands from the couch, where she's sitting with Ernesto.

"I've got it," Róise calls, crouched by the bassinet with her phone.

"On it!" Bianca's on her knees by the tree, her phone pointed at Sophie and Neri.

Bianca straightens and taps on her phone. "Sent it to the group chat."

"Me too." Róise sits with her legs crisscrossed, watching Neri and Sophie in fascinated wonder.

Miceli joins her. On the floor. The Don of the Genovese on the floor. I open my mouth to say something and then shut it. No, that's the old Aria, the one who allowed tradition and expectations build an invisible wall between herself and the man she loved.

And between her and her children. But no longer.

Catalina leans into Severu's side, her head on his shoulder. He hasn't moved more than two feet from his wife and baby all morning.

"Do we *have* to open presents?" Sal mutters from his chair, though everyone can see he's already wearing the navy robe Ilaria gave him.

"Tradition, *marito mio,*" she replies, handing him a cup of cinnamon spiced espresso.

The look my brother-in-law gives his wife could turn the Potomac into nothing but steam. He pulls Ilaria down beside him.

That's one couple I don't have to worry about anymore.

"Pretty sure the baby counts as everyone's favorite gift this year anyway," Miceli adds, sipping prosecco and looking suspiciously relaxed.

I smile. "I certainly don't mind waiting to open gifts but I doubt Neri is nearly as insouciant as the rest of us."

"What's a sociate?" Neri asks.

"It means you don't care if we wait to open gifts," Miceli teases.

Neri opens his mouth and then shuts it, his expression going from little boy to made man in training in the blink of an eye. My heart hurts, but there's nothing I can say. That's the way Enzo and I raised our sons."

Raff isn't Enzo though. And Giulia isn't me. They both drop to the floor by their children.

Raff grins at Neri. "Maybe you don't mind, but I do. I asked your mom for remote control car. Do you think she got it for me?"

Neri's eyes round. "You did?"

"Yes."

"Did you, mamma? Did you get papà a car like mine?"

Giulia ruffles Neri's hair. "Let's start opening gifts and see."

Everyone has a single gift for Saint Stephen's Day as is our tradition. Neri insists his father opens his first. And no one tells him that's not protocol. That Severu should because he's godfather.

And something inside me loosens.

"Don't you want to open yours first, Miceli asks?"

But Neri shakes his head with vehemence. "I want to see if papà got a toy to play with me."

"Oh, my heart." Candi's voice is soft, but I hear her.

And I smile.

She's so good for Angelo, the son of my heart. Enzo and I made our mistakes, but we loved our children. His poor excuse for parents cannot claim even that saving grace.

Giulia did indeed get Raff a remote control car, something neither me, nor Ilaria would ever have done for our husbands. But Sal would have played with Salvatore if Ilaria had.

Enzo would only have used his if he could conceive of a way to use it for training the boys.

I look over at Baby Enzo. "I just want to watch that little boy grow up spoiled rotten."

I don't realize I've said the words out loud until my son speaks.

"He will *not* be spoiled," Severu says automatically and then grimaces.

"No, he won't. He'll be loved," Catalina counters gently. "And he'll know it."

Severu's face clears and he nods. "And maybe a little spoiled."

It's my turn to think, *Oh, my heart*. But his words give me so much hope for the next generation. Yes, they have to be brought up to take their rightful place in our world, but my grandchildren don't have to do forego so much of what it means to be a child like my sons did.

Nerissa moves to sit beside the bassinet, resting one hand gently on the blanket. "He's going to grow up surrounded by love." She smiles warmly at Neri and Sohie. "They all will."

Sal lifts his mug. "And power."

I smile. Sal is still the man his father raised him to be, but for all the bad things he's done, he's also a good man. A man who knows how to love.

"And protection," Ilaria adds.

"And sass," Bianca says. "There's too much stubborn in the De Luca genes for any of these kids to go short of that."

A ripple of laughter rolls through the room.

Baby Enzo stirs, blinking up at the ceiling lights. He lets out a soft yawn, then a wobbly little coo.

Catalina reaches for her son.

Severu leans in, helping her pick him up and kisses her temple. "Best Christmas ever."

She nods.

Looking around at my family, I have no doubt we all agree.

Outside, snow begins to fall, turning the world white and still. Inside, the De Lucas gather close, bound by blood, loyalty, and love.

And at the center of it all, three beautiful children, their legacy already written in the family that brought them into the world. But what path that legacy will take for each of them?

That's a story for another day.

EPILOGUE 2: STILL US

I LARIA

The ocean crashes below our cliffside villa, its lullaby sweeping through the open windows along with the scent of salt, citrus, and the orange blossom perfume I've been wearing since we landed.

Sal calls it "dangerously distracting."

I call it *a reminder*.

That we're still here. Still *us*. After thirty-four years and countless storms.

We came to Lisbon to be alone. To breathe. To rediscover whatever part of ourselves got lost between mafia obligations and the ache of silence.

Turns out we're not lost at all. Just...overdue.

Sal walks out of the en-suite bathroom, barefoot and shirtless, drying his hands with a towel. His slacks ride low on his hips, and his hair is damp from the shower. He looks younger in this soft lighting, but the lines at the corners of his eyes tell our story better than any photograph ever could.

"You're staring," he says, voice low and smooth as port wine.

"You're worth staring at." I don't say it to flatter. I say it because it's true.

His eyes darken as he crosses the room, stopping at the foot of the bed. "You've been teasing me all day, *moglie*. Walking around in that sundress with nothing underneath."

I stretch like a cat, the silk robe I donned when we returned to the villa after a day of sightseeing, slipping from one shoulder. "We're in Portugal. I thought you liked tradition."

"I like you naked."

I laugh, and that's when he moves.

Sal climbs over me with deliberate control, not pouncing like the young man I married—but surrounding me, *claiming* me like the man who's earned every part of me. I inhale the scent of him—soap, salt air, and something purely masculine that's always been mine.

"I missed you," I whisper.

"I never left," he growls against my throat. "But I'm done letting the world steal my time with you."

His mouth finds mine, and everything else disappears.

The kiss is deep. Possessive. *Home.*

My robe slips away, and he trails his lips down my throat, across my chest, leaving a path of heat and worship. His hands—strong, calloused, familiar—spread my thighs as if he's parting the sea.

"You're wet for me already," he murmurs, thumb brushing my slick center. "Like always."

My breath stutters. "You still want me after all this time?"

His eyes blaze with quiet fury. "*Sempre.* You are still the most beautiful woman I've ever seen. And this body?" His hand cups my breast, reverent. "Is mine."

I arch beneath him, chasing the heat, the need, the ache that only he can ease.

He kisses his way down my belly, slow and unhurried, until he's between my thighs, lifting one leg over his shoulder as he tastes me with the practiced hunger of a man who's never forgotten what I like.

I cry out, hands tangling in his hair. "Sal!"

"Say it again," he demands, voice gravel and sin.

I do. Again. And again. Until my body bows and shatters for him.

He doesn't stop until I'm begging—*really* begging—and then he moves up my body, sliding inside me with one powerful thrust that fills every empty place inside me.

We move together like we always have—like fire and gravity, like storm and calm. Like we were made for this.

He wraps me in his arms, his thrusts deep and slow, like he's trying to imprint his soul on mine.

And maybe he does.

Because when we come together, it's not loud or fast—it's *forever*.

The smell of coffee draws me from sleep more gently than any alarm ever has. That, and the press of warm sunlight across my bare back through gauzy white curtains billowing in the ocean breeze.

I reach across the bed, but his side is empty—though still warm.

Slipping on Sal's button-down shirt from the night before, I pad barefoot out to the terrace.

He's there, of course.

Shirtless again. Gray streaks at his temples catching the rising light. A thick porcelain cup in his hand. Not his usual De Luca scowl, just a thoughtful crease between his brows as he stares out over the Atlantic.

When I wrap my arms around his middle from behind, he exhales softly and covers my hands with his.

"I didn't want to wake you."

"You didn't." I press a kiss to the space between his shoulder blades. "But I would've forgiven you for bringing me espresso in bed."

He chuckles and turns in my arms. "You'll have it now. Sit."

I do, curling into a cushioned wicker chair as he places a steaming cup in front of me and takes the seat beside me.

We sit in silence for a few minutes, sipping.

Listening.

Breathing.

It feels decadent, this stillness.

Like contraband.

"You look happy," he says, voice rough from sleep. Or emotion. Maybe both.

"I am." I tilt my face toward the rising sun. "It's different here. There's no weight in the air."

"No ghosts," he agrees quietly.

My fingers tighten around the warm ceramic. "We've lived a whole life, Sal. The kind people write about. Fight for. Die for."

His gaze drifts to the horizon. "I didn't always give you enough of it."

"You gave me everything that mattered. And now? Now you're giving me more."

He doesn't speak. Just takes my hand and lifts it to his mouth, pressing a kiss to skin that tingles from his touch.

"I was afraid," I whisper. "That we'd forgotten how to be just us."

His eyes meet mine, stormy and soft all at once. "We didn't forget. We just... paused. But we're unpausing now."

"Is that your official position, Consigliere?"

A rare smile cracks his stoic expression. "Yes. And if you're not convinced, I'll make a presentation later. With charts."

I laugh so hard I nearly spill my espresso.

When I lean in to kiss him, it's sweet and lazy. No rush. No desperation.

Just love.

Steady.

Ours.

Always.

THE END

ITALIAN & SICILIAN GLOSSARY

Note: certain words are not italicized in the book because of their common use in American English. Also, these translations are not literal. They are the more common vernacular. Italian as it is used in Northern or Southern Italy (and Sicily) as the case may be.

accidenti – (positive) wow, gosh, my goodness (negative) darn, drat

alla famiglia – to the family

amati/amate – beloved (m/f)

amata moglie – beloved wife

amore mio – my love

amorina – little love

amicu/amica – friend (m/f – Sicilian)

anima gemella – soul mate (no masculine form/same for either)

basta – stop, that's enough

bastardo – bastard

bèdda – beautiful (Sicilian)

biddùzza – beautiful (more endearing form Sicilian)

bella mia – you are my beautiful one, or listen to me i.e. in an argument to get the person's attention (alternate uses from Southern Italy)

bella ragazza – beautiful girl

bellissima - gorgeous

bisnonna – great grandmother

bisnonno – great grandfather

brava ragazza – good girl

bravo – well done

cara/o – darling

carina/o – cutie or pretty one

carissimo/a – very dear

cazzate – bullshit

cazzo – dick/fuck equivalent

caspita – yikes/wow

che bella – how beautiful

che bello – how handsome/how nice

che buono – how tasty

che palle – oh balls/fuck it equivalent

codardo – coward

cuore mio – my heart

dannazione – god damn it

delizia – when someone or something is yummy

Dio mio – my god

dolce fiore – sweet flower

dolce ragazza – sweet girl

dolcezza – sweetheart, honey (literally sweetness)

mamma – mom or mother

fottuto stronzo – fucking asshole (see also *stronzo del cazzo*)

fratello - brother

giamope – fool (Sicilian and credited with being the basis for *jamook/giamoke*)

gioia ru me core – joy of my heart (Sicilian)

goomah – mistress or side piece

grazie a Dio – thank God

il mia lei – my her (possessive endearment for a woman)

il mio lui – my him (possessive endearment for a man)

la mia dia – my goddess

il mio tutto – my everything

ma va' – no way

ma va? – really?

magari – I wish

mamma mia – oh, man
managgia – damn
managgia la miseria – damn it (literally misery or poverty)
manaja – damn (variant from Southern Italy)
marito – husband
meno male – thank goodness
mi vitù – my life (Sicilian)
moglie – wife
nonna – grandma/grandmother
nonno – grandpa/grandfather
oh merda – oh crap/shit
patatina – a small potato (it's a beautiful thing not like in English)
per favore – please
piccolo gatto – little cat
porca miseria – damn it
puffetta – it means a female Smurf
puttana – bitch
saluti – cheers (Sicilian)
sempre – always
sempre e per sempre – always and forever
stronzo/a – asshole (also another way to say bitch)
stronzo del cazzo – fucking asshole (see also *fottuto stronzo*)
tesoro – treasure
tesoro mio – my treasure
vaffanculo - fuck
vita mia – my life
vitù – (my) life in Sicilian
Phrases:
A accidenti. – (teasing or serious) darn him/her/you
Dammi il tuo cazzo. - give me your cock
Ho detto basta - that's enough, I said enough
Ho bisogno di te. – I need you.
Ho bisogno del tuo cazzo. – I need your cock.
Io sono tua. – I am yours.

Oh, sono qui! - Hey, I'm here.

Non fermarti! – Don't stop!

Prometto. – I promise.

Tu sei mia! –You are mine. (jealous: another man or woman involved)

Sei fuori! - Are you out of your mind?

Sei la mia anima gemelli. – You are my soul mate. (no masculine form – same for either)

Sei mio. – You are mine.

T'amu. – I love you. (Sicilian)

Ti amo. – I love you.

Ti perseguiterò per sempre. – I'll stalk you forever.

Uscire. - Get out.

Voglio il tuo cazzo. - I want your cock.

Zitto. - Shut up.

Sei il grande amore della mia vita. You are the love of my life.

USA Today bestselling and award-winning author **Lucy Monroe** has published over 90 romance novels, with more than 12.5 million copies in print worldwide. Her stories have been translated across the globe and span contemporary, historical, and paranormal subgenres—often with a twist of suspense, always with heart and heat.

After a successful career in traditional publishing, Lucy transitioned to indie and now writes the emotionally rich, spicy romances she's most passionate about—including her newest series, *Syndicate Rules*, which features morally gray mafia heroes, bold heroines, and all the danger, desire, and redemption readers crave.

A lifelong romance reader and story lover, Lucy enjoys connecting with fellow book lovers online. Her stories prove one thing above all: love conquers all... but not easily.

For info on her books and series extras, visit Lucy's website:
www.lucymonroe.com
Subscribe to her newsletter:
Substack: @lucymonroeauthor
Follow her on Social Media:
Facebook: LucyMonroe.Romance
Instagram: lucymonroeromance
Pinterest: lucymonroebooks
goodreads: Lucy Monroe
YouTube: @LucyMonroeBooks

SCORSOLINI BABY SCANDAL
THE REAL DEAL
WILD HEAT (Connected to Hot Alaska Nights - Not a Billio
HOT ALASKA NIGHTS
3 Brides for 3 Bad Boys Trilogy
RAND, COLTON & CARTER

Harlequin Presents

THE GREEK TYCOON'S ULTIMATUM
THE ITALIAN'S SUITABLE WIFE
THE BILLIONAIRE'S PREGNANT MISTRESS
THE SHEIKH'S BARTERED BRIDE
THE GREEK'S INNOCENT VIRGIN
BLACKMAILED INTO MARRIAGE
THE GREEK'S CHRISTMAS BABY
WEDDING VOW OF REVENGE
THE PRINCE'S VIRGIN WIFE
HIS ROYAL LOVE-CHILD
THE SCORSOLINI MARRIAGE BARGAIN
THE PLAYBOY'S SEDUCTION
PREGNANCY OF PASSION
THE SICILIAN'S MARRIAGE ARRANGEMENT
BOUGHT: THE GREEK'S BRIDE
TAKEN: THE SPANIARD'S VIRGIN
HOT DESERT NIGHTS
THE RANCHER'S RULES
'DDEN: THE BILLIONAIRE'S
'IRGIN PRINCESS
'R TO THE MILLIONAIRE
H'S SECRETARY MISTRESS
 LOVE-CHILD
 LOVER 2-IN-1 with
 COON'S INHERITED BRIDE

THE SHY BRIDE
THE GREEK'S PREGNANT LOVER
FOR DUTY'S SAKE
HEART OF A DESERT WARRIOR
NOT JUST THE GREEK'S WIFE
ONE NIGHT HEIR
PRINCE OF SECRETS
MILLION DOLLAR CHRISTMAS PROPOSAL
SHEIKH'S SCANDAL
AN HEIRESS FOR HIS EMPIRE
A VIRGIN FOR HIS PRIZE
2017 CHRISTMAS CODA: The Greek Tycoons
KOSTA'S CONVENIENT BRIDE
THE SPANIARD'S PLEASURABLE VENGEANCE
AFTER THE BILLIONAIRE'S WEDDING VOWS
QUEEN BY ROYAL APPOINTMENT
HIS MAJESTY'S HIDDEN HEIR
THE COST OF THEIR ROYAL FLING

Anthologies & Novellas

SILVER BELLA
DELICIOUS: Moon Magnetism
by Lori Foster, et. al.
HE'S THE ONE: Seducing Tabby
by Linda Lael Miller, et. al.
THE POWER OF LOVE: No Angel
by Lori Foster, et. al.
BODYGUARDS IN BED:
Who's Been Sleeping in my Brother's Bed?
by Lucy Monroe et. al.

Historical Romance

ANNABELLE'S COURTSHIP
The Langley Family Trilogy
TOUCH ME, TEMPT ME & TAKE ME
MASQUERADE IN EGYPT

Paranormal Romance

Children of the Moon Novels
MOON AWAKENING
MOON CRAVING
MOON BURNING
DRAGON'S MOON
ENTHRALLED anthology: Ecstasy Under the Moon
WARRIOR'S MOON
VIKING'S MOON
DESERT MOON
HIGHLANDER'S MOON

Montana Wolves
COME MOONRISE
MONTANA MOON